www.guideposts.org
Series Editor: Michele Slung
Cover art by Robert Tanenbaum
Cover design by Wendy Bass
Interior design by José R. Fonfrias
Interior cat illustrations by Viqui Maggio
Typeset by Composition Technologies, Inc.
Printed in the United States of America

*Dedicated with love and admiration to Pat Furlong
and Glynne Turner
for their enthusiasm, advice and support.
Special thanks to Elizabeth Kramer Gold and Michele Slung.*

1

S O WHEN'S THE PRECIOUS bundle coming home?"
Gracie Parks leaned forward in her kitchen chair,
listening intently. It had been raining in Willow Bend for
days and she was anxious for some soul-lifting news. "This
afternoon! My goodness, Nancy, they're out of the hospital
quickly these days, aren't they?"

The voice on the other end of the telephone line laughed.
"Not like in our day, no siree." Nancy Bixler continued, "In
and out like clockwork, that's the modern way. Of course, it
being her second child, Phyllis knows what she's in for."
Nancy was a nurse, as well as a mother, and she knew all too
well.

Gracie heard a booming sound in the background. "Sorry,
hon," Nancy added, her voice suddenly pitched higher.
"Incoming patients, got to run. Take care and give my love to
Uncle Miltie."

Gracie assured Nancy that she would and replaced the receiver. Though delighted for the Nickolsons, Gracie couldn't help feeling a titch lonely. It had been too long since she'd held a newborn and inhaled its powdery-fresh scent. She reached for her coffee, only to find it stone cold. Sighing, Gracie walked to the kitchen sink and stared through the fat raindrops clinging to the window. Of course, the garden needed the precipitation, but as her eyes trailed along the post and rail fence, she focused on her prized ivory tulips. Much more hard rain and they might need staking.

The charcoal skies darkened. With a thunderous *boom!* the heavens split. Water roared down, drumming against the roof of her two-story clapboard. She watched the white vaselike flower heads droop alarmingly. Even God seems under the weather, she thought.

Gracie's large, airy kitchen was quiet. Gooseberry, her Halloween-colored tomcat, had disappeared at first light, his dish still full of food. Her eighty-year-old uncle, George Morgan, fondly nicknamed Uncle Miltie because of his terrible jokes, was at the Willow Bend seniors center, no doubt cleaning up at pinochle. Having Uncle Miltie stay with her since his wife had passed away over two years ago was a blessing, although she continued to miss her dear husband, Elmo. More than five years had passed since his fatal accident and she still thought of him daily.

As the coffeepot gurgled, she recalled the brilliant

sunshine so many years ago into which she and Elmo had carried their only child, Arlen. Oh, they had been so happy! So young and blessed! Elmo's large hands had been shaking when he first held their dark-haired miracle, his voice thick with wonder as he thanked God and Gracie for their bounty. She smiled at a nearby family photo and vowed to give her son a call. He now lived in New York City with his wife, Wendy, and their young son, Elmo.

"Dear Lord," she whispered, "help me count my blessings and keep in mind to use Your precious gifts in Your name." For a minute, she listened to the uneven patter on the roof, its tattoo softer now, as the idea drifted into her head. "A cake!" she exclaimed, reaching for her *Thyme for God, Thyme for Study, Thyme for Prayer* apron. "Of course. I'll bake a homecoming cake for Phyllis's brand-new boy."

Within minutes, the clouds in her head lifted just as the sun crept into view beyond her window. She had examined the contents of her well-stocked freezer, refrigerator and pantry, and was in the middle of stirring the batter for a strawberry and custard swirl cake when the screen door yawned. In a flash, Gooseberry curled through her legs and headed to his dish, followed by a beaming Uncle Miltie. Slightly crippled by osteoarthritis, the octogenarian maneuvered his aluminum walker carefully through the doorway. Steadying himself, he thrust his gnarled hands into his pockets and shook them violently. The resulting rattle made

Gracie laugh out loud. "I take it you won, then?" she said, affectionately touching his arm, feeling her spirits rise at the pair's return.

"Is Willow Bend in Indiana?" he replied, blue eyes flashing. He hesitated then sniffed knowingly. "That smells mighty good, dear. Any chance there's a cuppa Joe for an old champ like me?"

The screen door creaked again. Marge Lawrence, their next-door neighbor and Gracie's best friend, popped her perfectly coiffed head through the entrance asking, "Is that fresh coffee?"

"Come on in," Uncle Miltie replied. "We may even scrounge a molasses cookie or two."

"Opening late?" Gracie asked. Marge owned a gift shop in town. Sometimes Gracie felt the best gift of all was the freedom the shop offered her friend, as its hours were a little unconventional. A bit like her friend.

Marge tugged at an earring which resembled a dangling clump of gold and grinned. "The perks of small business."

As Marge pulled out mugs and poured the coffee, Gracie finished beating the cake batter, poured it into two tins and pushed them into the oven. Marge handed her a steaming mug while Uncle Miltie carried the large crockery cookie jar to the table. Gracie listened and chuckled as her uncle recounted his pinochle-winning ways. Gooseberry leapt into her lap, licked the inside of her arm and then, purring loudly, curled carefully into a ball.

"We're thinking of organizing a little something at the center," Uncle Miltie said, reaching for a cookie. "The guys suggested that you might consider getting involved."

Marge stroked her upswept curls. "If I were you, Gracie Parks, I'd hightail it out of here right this minute. Who knows what these men are up to?" She winked broadly, and continued, her voice light with teasing. "Probably want to introduce strip pinochle or some such foolishness."

While her uncle faked a frown, Gracie managed to sip her coffee and hide the smile threatening to dance across her face. She could almost guess what was coming. Gracie and her husband had often volunteered at the seniors' center. Gracie presided over the kitchen, while Elmo, a whiz at organizing and involving others, always had managed to include every senior in some entertaining or informative activity. Her husband's fund-raising successes at the Mason County Fair were also legendary, raising a great bounty for the center, charities, and local churches, including their own, the Eternal Hope Community Church. Several of his events, including bovine bingo, combine racing, and the fence-post pitch, were continued to this day. Elmo's popularity and honesty had been two of the main reasons he was later voted in with an overwhelming majority as the town mayor. Gently shifting aside the bittersweet thoughts of the past, Gracie embraced the present and nodded at her uncle.

Tossing Marge a dark look, Uncle Miltie continued, "We thought we'd create a permanent display honoring the war veterans from Willow Bend. Have a standing invitation to the schools. You know, show some of the youngsters our finest hour, as Churchill would say. They all think we're just old and useless." Gracie patted his arm encouragingly as he continued, "Wondered if you might consider bringing a few members of the choir to help set up. Maybe join in a sing-along?" Gracie and Marge were both longtime members of the Eternal Hope Community Church's choir which often sang at benefits and other civic events. Uncle Miltie cleared his throat. "And would you consider catering desserts for our opening? The center could pay, I'm sure."

Gracie's hand stopped in mid-air and she blinked. "That's a wonderful idea!" She set down her mug with a thud. "We could even come up with wartime-era treats." She glanced at her best friend, her eyes twinkling. "What do you think, Marge, some fake cocoa and a Spam loaf?"

Marge laughed, as her dangling earrings bounced. "That will sure bring back the memories. I think I've got an old matching skirt and sweater set. Perfect for the occasion."

"Wish I could fit into something that old," Gracie sighed, stroking Gooseberry's chin. "So when is this noble and nostalgic event?"

Uncle Miltie bit into another cookie and munched for a moment. "Depends on you, dear. It will take us a few days to go through our photos and what-not, but I wasn't sure about your schedule. You know . . . for the catering."

Gracie smiled. "You know I'm happy to do it—let me just look at my calendar."

He nodded. "Whatever suits you, my dear, tickles me plum to death." Marge chuckled. Uncle Miltie leaned back. "It's so hard to get today's youth interested in the events of the past. Everybody's in such a gall-darned hurry these days—what with their dot com this and WWW that. Don't know what they're even talking about most of the time." He raked his fingers through his thick gray hair. "Perhaps this will help the whippersnappers to remember the WW's of other generations. Without them, my dears, life'd sure be different."

"Amen to that," Marge replied heartily, brushing cookie crumbs off her lips.

Gracie carefully put Gooseberry onto his favorite chair by the kitchen door, then began checking her cakes. "It will be fun—"

The telephone rang.

Gracie excused herself, smoothed her hands on her apron and then picked up the phone. "Hello?"

"Gracie!" a woman's excited voice jumped through the receiver. It was Anna Searfoss, who, along with her husband Joe, had been one of the founding members of Eternal Hope.

"Anna? Is everything all right?" Gracie's stomach knotted. She often worried about her dear friend, a retired librarian who was nearly blind and suffering from diabetes.

"What? Oh, yes! Yes." Gracie's heart soared at the fresh strength she could hear in Anna's voice. "We have wonderful news, Gracie. Just wonderful! I can't wait to tell you. When can you come over?"

"Uh," Gracie replied, switching gears quickly, "how about a half hour?"

"Bring Uncle Miltie," Anna added. "And Marge if you can find her." Gracie grinned.

Both her uncle and best friend were talking at her as she hung up the phone. Gracie raised a hand. "It's Anna! *Very* excited. She's asked us over to hear some great news."

"Then, why are you frowning?" Uncle Miltie asked.

Gracie glanced at the kitchen clock. "Hope you don't mind postponing the rest of the discussion. I think I need to check the freezer while these cake layers finish baking. I want to make sure I have a proper treat to accompany Anna's surprise."

C OME IN! COME IN," Joe Searfoss said, pulling open the front door. Gracie, holding an apple crisp, stepped inside.

"We've brought dessert," Uncle Miltie declared, stomping up the steps after the others.

"And we've got tidings of great joy!" Joe replied, moving aside.

"Come in! Come in!" Anna's voice happily exclaimed from the kitchen. "How good of you to come."

The foursome followed the smell of freshly brewed coffee and trooped into the Searfosses' small, neat-as-a-pin kitchen. Gracie placed the still-steaming dessert on the table.

"That smells wonderful," Anna said. "Apple?"

"Apple Gracie, right out of the freezer and into the oven,"

Marge replied, giving Anna's shoulder a squeeze. "Low in sugar but chockablock with sultana raisins and bran flakes."

"Thank you, dear," Anna said. "It was kind of you to think of making our announcement even more festive. Joe and I, we're so excited, we couldn't cook."

"Excited about what?" Marge asked, grabbing plates and cutlery off the counter and quickly setting four places.

"Please," Joe said. "Take a seat. Coffee everyone?"

They all nodded and sat down. Joe handed out the coffee, cream and sugar, then settled beside his wife. He squeezed her hand and said, "You tell them, dear. It's really *your* news."

"Will *somebody* please spill the beans?" Uncle Miltie demanded. "I'm not getting any younger, you know."

Anna put her free hand over that of her husband's. "How fortunate we are to have such good friends to share this with." She took a deep breath. Uncle Miltie leaned forward. "My children's books about Scotty and Suzy, the Sandersons of Lazy Lake, you remember?" Gracie nodded, then touched her friend's frail hand as acknowledgment. A lovely smile brightened the lines radiating across Anna's oval face. "Well, an editor at a New York publishing house—a very nice woman—called out of the blue a few months ago. Didn't she, Joe?" He nodded while she continued. "It seems she read my Lazy Lake stories when she was a child. She told me that their small-town setting was—how did she put it, Joe?"

16

"Ripe."

Anna smiled again. "That's it. *Ripe* for reissuing. Well, the Lord has answered my prayers. She just called. The books are going to be reprinted."

Uncle Miltie let out a joyous whoop. "Such sweet news definitely calls for something sweet to eat!" Gracie and Marge jumped up and embraced both the Searfosses, questions tumbling from their mouths. As Joe and Anna excitedly explained, Gracie clasped her hands together and happily watched the animated expressions glowing on the faces of her uncle and friends. Marge served each of them a generous helping of crisp which they immediately tasted. "Anyone for cream?"

"Oh, this is good!" Joe said.

"Lovely," Anna added. "Just the right amount of cinnamon."

They ate happily.

A couple of minutes later, Anna's expression darkened and her voice dropped to a whisper. "I must confess, when we first heard, I . . . I was overcome with sadness." Her unseeing eyes filled with tears. "No family with whom to share the good news." Her husband softly brushed her cheek. Gracie tugged free a couple of tissues from her purse and put them into Anna's hand. "My dear sister and brother-in-law . . . both called to God years ago." Anna's voice caught but she struggled on. "And young Tommy—I think that's the hardest of all."

"Where is he?" Marge asked.

"Oh, dear. That's another tragedy," Anna whispered. "We lost touch. That sweet boy was like my very own." Joe nodded. "We spent every summer together until he was eight. Then my sister died and her husband—a military man—couldn't take care of him. So Tommy was raised by his grandparents." She paused, thinking. "Why, he'd be over forty by now." Anna swallowed hard then said, "This wonderful news and no family to share it with." Anna's face lit up. "But then my Joe said that it was nonsense. That we weren't alone! That we had all of you and so many others. . . ." The tears flowed again. Uncle Miltie blinked furiously and Marge reached for her own hankie.

No one spoke, but Gracie understood exactly how Anna felt. Wondering how, for even a moment, she could have been feeling a little blue and lonely when she was truly blessed by having these fine people in her life, Gracie Parks whispered a short prayer of thanks.

3

"THAT'S MY CAKE, RIGHT?" the young girl said, tugging violently at her chestnut pigtail. She yanked the door fully open to welcome Gracie.

Gracie stood on the step, strawberry custard swirl cake in hand, blinking in the mid-morning sunlight at the slender girl. "It's to celebrate the birth of your new baby brother. For *all* of you, young lady."

"Same diff. Because *the precious one* can't eat cake," the girl added with backward glance. "*It* hasn't any teeth." She grinned briefly, flashing a trestle of silver braces.

A woman's voice floated from inside. "Who is it, Katie? Oh, it's you, Gracie!" Patting a diapered, sleeping infant on her shoulder, Phyllis Nickolson approached the entrance. Gracie noticed the fatigue in her friend's freckled face and couldn't help feeling sorry for the woman. She remembered only too well how little sleep one gets around newborns.

"How nice to see you," Phyllis said, her normally booming voice pitched more softly than usual. "Katie! Where're your manners, child? Invite Mrs. Parks in."

The girl reluctantly stood by while Gracie edged inside the narrow hallway, cluttered with stuffed toys, baby gear and shoes. "I hope you don't mind my coming unannounced, but Nancy told me you were bringing home the baby yesterday. I wanted to be among the first to welcome your newest blessing."

"How kind of you!" Phyllis exclaimed. Her dark eyes lit up at seeing the dessert. "You shouldn't have." She patted the baby's back softly then chuckled. "Must admit, though, it'll be greatly appreciated. Haven't done much in the kitchen these last few weeks, what with backaches, swollen feet . . . you know how it is." Phyllis rolled her eyes. "Come through here with me, and please, excuse the mess." They picked their way down the hall to a large, bright yellow kitchen. Gracie took a deep breath. The counters were littered with unwashed dishes, baby bottles and an open jug of milk.

Pushing aside some plates, Gracie placed the cake on the counter. She popped the milk into the fridge then with a brisk smile, assisted Phyllis into a straight-backed chair. "So this is Darren."

Phyllis nodded, gently turning the baby. His blue eyes fluttered weakly. "Darren Michael, after Terry's father."

She carefully handed the baby to Gracie. Struck by his

diminutive size and soft smell, Gracie cooed appreciatively and stroked Darren's fine pale fuzz. Her own Arlen had been blessed with a thatch of black hair, just like his father's. The baby's hand gripped her finger and she smiled. Truly one of God's greatest miracles! Though barely home from the hospital, the newly minted Nickolson was beautiful, his tiny face plumper than most newborns. "He's gorgeous." She gingerly returned him to his mother's arms. Ignoring the urge to start tidying up, Gracie dropped into a chair. "Darren Michael Nickolson's a lovely name. Very strong."

"Izz not. Izz not. It's stupid, stupid!" Katie shrieked, skipping suddenly into the room. "Daaarrrren!" she cried in a sing-song voice. "Dumb-dumb, dumb-dumb Daaarrrren!"

"Katie!" Phyllis snapped. "Please, honey. Don't say things like tha—"

The baby's tiny face scrunched then he started to wail.

"Oooh no . . . not again." Phyllis held Darren, now furiously squawking, in her arms and began softly rocking him. Katie continued to skip around the kitchen table, shouting, "Watch me skip, Mommy. Watch *me!*"

Over the baby's howling and Katie's trumpeting, Phyllis cried, "Katie, please!"

Gracie waited until the little girl passed by her then snatched quickly and grabbed Katie's arm. "Wait a minute, young lady," she said sternly, pulling the skipper toward her. "You're scaring your little brother."

"So what?" Katie asked, yanking her arm free. "All he ever does is cry. Cried in the hospital, in the car. He always cries."

Gracie looked directly into the girl's eyes. "If you will behave yourself, you may have a piece of my special cake." Continuing to rock the sobbing baby, Phyllis shot her an appreciative glance.

Katie eyed her doubtfully. "What kind is it? Has it got coconut? I *hate* coconut. Only monkeys eat coconut."

Gracie smiled and stood up. "Not one teensy little flake. Come on, I'll even let you do the slicing."

Within a couple of minutes, Katie was seated, happily alternating between bites of cake and sips of milk. "Strawberries," she exclaimed, licking her lips. "My fave."

Darren had fallen asleep, so as Phyllis gently placed him face down in a nearby bassinet, Gracie made coffee and cut two small slices of the strawberry custard swirl.

"How long before you have to return to work at the hospital?" Gracie asked, pouring coffee.

"Six months," Phyllis replied, setting their plates at the table. "At least, that's what I'm entitled to."

"I don't know what they are going to do without you," Gracie said. "You are the best at the switchboard." She took a bite. *Not bad.* She chewed thoughtfully. *Perhaps a bit more vanilla next time?* "I remember once last year, you weren't in, and your replacement put me through to Pre-Natal when I asked for Doctor Peter Natalie's office."

Phyllis chuckled and almost choked on a sip of coffee. "That must have been Bernice," she sputtered. "Nice woman, but a little hard of hearing."

Katie shoved her plate aside and jumped up. "I'm going outside. Want to see me ride my new bike?"

"Let Mrs. Parks finish her coffee and cake, all right, honey? We're going to chat for a while." The girl's face darkened. Her mother looked across at Gracie and raised her eyebrows in a pleading gesture. "Perhaps she can see you ride on her way out."

Gracie placed her fork on her plate. "I'd love to, Katie. You go on outside. I'll join you a little later."

"Oh, all right," the girl replied, then skipped out of the room. Gracie noticed that she didn't take her dishes to the counter but said nothing. Obviously, Phyllis was spoiling the child.

Phyllis sank back into her chair and exhaled heavily. "Thanks. I really don't know what to do with that child. Just bought her the bike, you know, to make her feel special?" Gracie nodded. "Something to take her mind off . . ." Phyllis ran a hand through her loose hair. "It was hard enough for her to adapt to Terry. She still won't call him Dad, but . . ." she reached across and stroked Darren's neck. "This little guy's really thrown her for a loop."

Gracie finished her last morsel of cake. "None of us adapts well to change, especially children. It just takes time and lots of love." She smiled at her friend. "There's no doubt she's getting the latter. I'll say a prayer or two." She took a sip of coffee. Phyllis nodded her thanks. "A little time, we'll all settle into a new routine. Terry's a bit spooked himself." She blushed faintly, her freckles rising to the surface. "Darren's his first, so he's not had too much experience with babies."

Gracie stood and took their dishes to the sink. "A few diaper changes and he'll be an expert." They both laughed. "Well, I really must be off. Uncle Miltie will be wondering what happened to me."

"Thank you so much for coming," Phyllis said. "Terry will be disappointed he missed you, but he'll enjoy your wonderful cake. Hope you don't mind," she added, glancing toward the bassinet, "if I don't see you out."

"Not at all." Gracie wanted to say that she could come by another day and tidy up a bit but feared her friend might be embarrassed. "I'll give you a call in a day or so to see how you're doing."

Outside, Katie was wheeling around the sidewalk, her skinny legs whirling the pedals of a shiny red bicycle. "See, Mrs. Parks?" the girl shouted, removing a hand from the bars.

"No, dear!" Gracie cried out, breaking into a sprint down the steps.

The girl waved then let go with the other hand. Immediately, the bike bobbled. "No hands—oooh!"

Afterward, Gracie was certain she'd been given a divine push. There was no other possible explanation as to how she'd managed to cover those few feet in an instant but, suddenly, there she was, clutching the bike with one hand and wrapping her arm around the girl with the other.

"You're okay, Katie," she murmured into the startled girl's hair. She realized she was out of breath. "The good Lord was watching." She smiled at the thought. "He always is."

"Nothing's wrong, dear," Gracie said into the phone, later that evening. "I just wanted to know how you were." After seeing Phyllis's new baby and miraculously rescuing Katie from a nasty spill, Gracie Parks needed to hear her own son's voice. To make sure that he, his wife, and her precious little grandson, Elmo, were safe.

"We're all fine, Mom," Arlen replied. "Same old, same old. Work's hectic but good. Elmo's growing like a weed."

A boy's voice shouted in the background, "Not a *weed*, Dad! Like one of Gramma's sunflowers."

Arlen chuckled. "Did you hear that?"

Gracie laughed. "I sure did." She filled her son in on the latest happenings: the newest citizen of Willow Bend, Uncle Miltie's gambling wins, and the plans for the seniors center upcoming memorial display. She had agreed with Uncle Miltie and the center's staff to cater dessert for the event in just over two weeks. "I realize it's short notice, dear, but any chance you could come? It'd be good for Elmo to know about his great-great uncle's role in the war."

"Wish we could, Mom!" Arlen replied. Gooseberry chose that very moment to jump off a kitchen chair and, tail arched, bumped her leg with a purring caress. She ruffled his black stripes affectionately. "Things are a little hectic . . ." Arlen was saying. "Look, if we don't get there for the opening night, it'll be on display for a while, right?"

"Oh, yes. It's planned to be permanent."

"Great! There's no rush, then. We'll see it on our next visit. Give my best to Uncle Miltie. We love you!"

"Hugs and kisses to all of you. God bless," Gracie replied, hanging up, bestowing one of each on Gooseberry.

A COUPLE OF QUIET WEEKS rolled by with nothing new to talk about other than the late spring ridge of high pressure which had slowly edged over Willow Bend. Hot winds billowed along the main streets and slipped into residents' homes. Each day, as the temperature crept higher, the citizens fanned their flushed faces and prayed for relief. Uncle Miltie wasn't at all surprised. In fact, having consulted his *Farmer's Almanac* as usual, he had already switched his wardrobe of button cardigans and long-sleeved shirts for suspenders and short sleeves.

To beat the heat, Gracie had begun rising earlier and praise-walking just as the reddish-gold streaks of new light flashed across the Indiana horizon. She walked to think, to be closer to God and, it must be admitted, to try and maintain her weight. Fortunately, she enjoyed many ancillary benefits of her daily exercise. This particular cloudless May morning, Gracie had marveled at the dawn kaleidoscope and relished the heady aromatic mix of grass clippings, wet earth and early peonies.

Upon her return, Gracie had received a call from Anna Searfoss, inviting her to drop by that morning. After she hung up, she had quickly started on a batch of raisin scones to take, using whole wheat flour for the first time.

"Don't you think someone ought to taste them before you take them to Anna's?" Uncle Miltie said, blinking innocently at his niece.

Even though he'd earlier enjoyed sharing a large plate of parsley-scrambled eggs with Gracie, Uncle Miltie eyed the batch of steaming biscuits from his kitchen chair. Gooseberry yawned from his place atop the fridge. "After all, you did say it was a new recipe," he said, nursing a last cup of coffee. "Your reputation's at stake, you know."

Gracie glanced at her watch and smiled. "I can't argue with that, but you're on your own, since I'll be having one with Anna. You might want the strawberry preserves, though. For Anna's sake, the scones have no sugar. I'll get a plate."

While Uncle Miltie clumped to the pantry, dropped a jar into the mesh basket dangling from his walker and returned to his seat, Gracie popped two scones onto a small plate, rummaged in the flatware drawer for a knife and set them on the table.

It took Uncle Miltie slightly less time to slice, spread and taste the first scone than it took Gracie to refill his mug with coffee.

"Mouth-watering," he drawled, licking his fingers. "These're even better than the last ones and *they* were tastier than the ones before that. What'd you do different this time besides cutting out the sugar?"

Gracie took a sip from her coffee cup and grimaced. Lukewarm. She stood up, rinsed the mug and put it in the dishwasher along with the breakfast dishes. "It's the flour. I used whole-wheat. It gives them a nice texture and marbled color, don't you think?"

"Can't say as I notice texture or color, my dear, but the taste!" He launched into the second biscuit and munched happily. "Have you decided on the treats for the memorial display set-up?" He paused. "You're not really going to serve a Spam loaf?"

Gracie laughed, while removing the last batch of scones "How about deep-dish apricot cobbler, my special brownies, and hot-milk sponge cake?"

Her uncle rubbed his hands together. "Just the ticket."

She smiled. "I'll remind the choir to come and help out. I'm not sure how many can make it, but I know they'll try."

"That's grand. I'll tell the guys at the barber shop to skip dessert before coming."

"Barber shop?"

"Oh, didn't I say? That's why I can't join you at Anna's. Got to get my hair cut. I'm counting on you to tell me everything." He took a final gulp of coffee. "Any chance for a lift?"

"Of course. You can hold the scones, they're a bit warm to be wrapped up . . . " she paused and gave her uncle a long stare. "So long as the same number arrive as depart." Gooseberry rapidly flicked his tail.

The old man held up two gnarled fists. "These are the hands God trusted to defend our nation, dearie. I think they'll do right by your scones."

Gracie paused, uncertain as to whether she'd hurt Uncle Miltie's feelings. Then, a smile joined the lines on his face. She walked over and gave him a kiss on the cheek. He'd missed a spot shaving, but she didn't say anything.

"What's that for?" he said gruffly though she knew he was pleased.

"A little thank you. I don't think I say it often enough."

The World War II veteran blushed.

An hour later, Gracie was sitting in Anna Searfoss's living room, an old hardcover book cupped gently in her own hands. The morning light flooded across the Searfosses'

hardwood floors, bathing her friend in a golden halo. Gracie had arrived at Anna's home an hour earlier, freshly baked scones in hand. After enjoying orange pekoe tea with the scones, liberally spread with Anna's famous sugar-free bumbleberry jam, the two women had just moved from the kitchen to the living room.

Generally, Gracie was astonished by Anna's ability to negotiate her tidy home. Although nearly blind, Anna Searfoss, had a librarian's orderly mind and had an uncanny understanding of where each bit of dishware or piece of furniture lay. Gracie knew that her friend used a white cane when she occasionally ventured outside her home, but by eschewing rugs and keeping the furniture in the same places, the elderly woman usually moved about her own little castle with remarkable aplomb. Today, however, she had surprised both herself and Gracie by bumping the couch on the way to a sidetable. Gracie pretended not to notice. Still, once there, Anna had confidently reached out, avoiding an old photograph of Joe in front of his delivery truck, and proudly took a book from a pile to show Gracie.

Though faded, the book cover depicting a stand of massive fir trees towering over a mountain lake was a delightful combination of forest green and robin's-egg blue with cream trim. "*The Fishing Derby at Lazy Lake*, by Anna Searfoss. Why, it's lovely, Anna! Makes me want to go back in time, to see Indiana in the early days."

Her friend smiled shyly, gesturing toward the stack of books then fanned her face with a hand. "I'm sorry it's so warm in here. I need to get Joe to turn on the air conditioning." She looked a little sheepish. "I don't know how. We've just had it installed as a kind of a present to ourselves."

"Your timing couldn't be better," Gracie said. "As Uncle Miltie says, this heat wave's sticking like yesterday's oatmeal." She flipped to the back cover and read, a smile warming her face. "The turn of the century, what a wonderful period." She reached for another volume, *The Easter Egg Hunt at Lazy Lake*, and was immediately delighted by its violet, pink and silver motif. "I'd forgotten how truly lovely the covers were. Do you think they'll use the same ones or come up with something new?"

"I've no idea," Anna replied, settling into her overstuffed chair. She quickly felt the hands on her specially designed wristwatch. "I don't think I have much choice in the matter but I'm hoping they'll respect the original designs, perhaps just update them a little." Anna clasped a book to her bosom. "It's really very exciting, talking about my stories once again. Thinking of how many new children will get to know my Scotty and Suzy."

"It's going to be wonderful. Really wonderful. And speaking of new readers," Gracie said, "I visited Phyllis Nickolson yesterday and welcomed home her new baby, Darren

Michael." She paused, thinking of Katie. "He's a beautiful boy . . ." her voice trailed off.

Anna frowned. "What's wrong?"

Gracie smiled and touched her friend's hand. "Nothing slips by you, Anna." She hesitated, getting her thoughts together. "It's just . . . well, you know Phyllis has a daughter, Katie, from her first marriage?" Anna nodded. "It seems Katie's having a difficult time. First, in accepting a new father, and now, a new brother." Gracie shook her curls. "She's demanding a lot of attention and I wonder if Phyllis can handle it—"

The front door opened. Anna jumped in her seat as her husband called out, "Is he here yet?" Joe Searfoss was in the living room before his wife could respond. His face fell when he spied Gracie. "Oh, it's you," he said, clearly disappointed.

Gracie hesitated, struck dumb by his odd reaction.

"Oh, dear!" Joe added immediately, rushing over to embrace her. "I'm so sorry, Gracie. I didn't mean to be rude." He glanced at his wife. "It's just that we're expecting . . ."

Still embarrassed, Gracie stood. "I didn't realize. I really must be going."

"No! No," Anna cried out. "I was just going to tell you. It's really why I invited you over. Joe, please—"

"Yes, Gracie. You must stay. Forgive me!" He encouraged Gracie to sit. "We're a little muddled, aren't we, Anna?"

Anna smiled broadly. "I guess I should have told you when you came, but I wanted Joe to be with us. The Lord's blessed us a second time, Gracie. We've more wonderful news, haven't we, Joe?"

"Really?" Gracie replied. "About the books?"

"No. Better. Much better." Anna held out her hands, one to Gracie and the other to her husband. Gripping tightly, she continued, "It's a miracle."

"We received a phone call," Joe jumped in excitedly.

"From our nephew, Tommy," Anna added.

Gracie blinked. "Your ... nephew? I thought ... oh ... your sister's son? The one raised by his grandparents?" Anna beamed. "Why, that's ... that's wonderful news!" Gracie said, throwing her free arm around her friend.

"He saw a wire-service article about my books," Anna continued. "Recognized my picture and called up right away!" She squeezed Gracie's hand vigorously. "Best of all, he'll be here any second."

"Any sec—" Gracie stood, releasing her hand. "I'd better—"

"No!" Joe exclaimed. "Stay. We want you to stay."

"But this ... no, I couldn't."

The doorbell rang.

"I'll get it," Joe said, rising quickly.

5

ANNA REACHED OUT for the tall man, dressed in tan pants and a blue checked shirt, who followed Joe into their living room.

Gracie blinked, barely able to believe her eyes. *Why, this whole thing was like something from the Saturday afternoon movies Elmo had loved!* She eyed the stranger's shoes. Her father used to say you could tell a whole lot from a man's footwear. Sherlock Holmes, one of Gracie's favorite detectives, agreed. At first, she didn't know what to make of his scuffed, brown loafers, other than that they hadn't been polished in a while. After a moment, she guessed that he was unmarried. Also, a wife might have made him put on socks.

"Tommy . . . Thomas Joseph Williams, is it really you? Dear Lord, I've prayed but . . ."

The man bent, took Anna's hand and held it tenderly. "It's really me, auntie. In the flesh. Though everyone calls me Tom, now. I'm so glad to find you and Uncle Joe again."

Joe motioned toward Gracie. "This is our dear friend, Gracie Parks."

"Pleased to meet you, ma'am," Tom replied. "Any friend of my aunt and uncle's is a friend of mine."

Gracie shook his hand politely and retreated a bit, the better to study the visitor further. Slightly built with a nervous air, he seemed to be in his early forties. His bright-blue eyes set off a face framed by unruly brown hair.

Joe motioned for Tom to sit. He perched on the edge of the chair, left foot twitching.

"You have a lovely voice, Tommy," Anna said. "Very strong. You used to sing beautifully. Do you remember? We'd hold hands, go to church." Her face brightened. "You loved 'Let the River Flow.'"

Tom looked blank for a moment, then smiled. "Of course, right!" He laughed uncomfortably. "I . . . I was pretty young," he said, glancing at Joe and Gracie. "Don't really remember much, I'm afraid."

"Makes sense," Joe said heartily. "After all, you were just a kid."

Anna raised her hands. "May I?"

For a moment, Tom looked confused then knelt in front of her. "Oh, of course!"

Anna gently ran her fingertips over his narrow face. When Anna finished, she sat quietly for a moment, her face a window on her memories. Gracie began to feel uncomfortable, certain she was intruding on a very personal experience. She knew she should leave, that this was a private matter, but couldn't seem to find the right words.

"Please, Tommy, er, Tom, sit back down," Joe instructed.

"Thank you." Once again, the tall stranger sat across from his aunt.

Gracie was struck by the bundle of energies radiating from the trio. It reminded her of the sensations sweeping her choir just before a big event: a high-pitched buzz, a rumbling tremor and a giddy sense of relief. Waiting, she inhaled deeply.

There was a moment of awkward silence then Joe, Anna and Tom spoke simultaneously. They stopped and then laughed, again as one. "You first, Auntie Anna," Tom said.

"Oh, there's so much racing through my head. I can hardly think." She paused, her forehead wrinkling. "Tell us about yourself, Tommy. I want to know everything. We're *so* thankful you found us, aren't we, Joe?"

Tom Williams nodded, a lock of hair bouncing across his forehead. "Same here. It's funny, huh? Just happened to see a news article on the reprinting of a series of popular children's books by an Indiana author named Anna Searfoss. The name meant something to me, I knew . . ." he frowned, then rushed on. "There was something familiar about the book titles and *then* I looked at the picture." He reached across to squeeze his aunt's hand. "*Bang!* It was like a light bulb bursting in my head."

Shaking her head slightly, Anna softly rubbed his long fingers. "It's been so long, Tommy. We'd pretty well given up hope of ever finding you, hadn't we, Joe? What luck—no, not luck, *divine intervention*, that my little books would bring you to me."

Anna's words brought Gracie up sharply. Could family affection be the sole reason this man had turned up? But she immediately chided herself. *Fiddlesticks, Gracie! You've been reading one too many Agatha Christies!* What could it mean, anyway?

"And your family . . . are you married?" Anna asked.

Tom shook his head, then remembering his aunt's disability and replied in the negative. "But enough about me! I want to know all about you and Uncle Joe."

For a few minutes, Anna and Joe chatted excitedly, their faces glowing. Then, Joe asked Tom what he did for a living.

"Oh," the newcomer replied, breezily, scooping up the old photograph of Joe. "Nothing as hands on as this." He poked the picture. "You still enjoy driving, Uncle Joe?"

The way Tom Williams had deflected his uncle's innocent question bothered Gracie. Ignoring the little voice in her head that was telling her not to seek out trouble, she forced herself to concentrate, to listen and watch very carefully. Why she felt something seemed wrong with this picture wasn't clear to her. Yet something about the reunion she was seeing felt *odd* to Gracie. She fretted inwardly.

Joe smiled ruefully. "Not so much, anymore. Folks always rushing, honking their horns. Not like the old days."

Gracie couldn't contain her tiny doubts any longer. The

timing of Tom Williams's arrival, on the heels of Anna's wonderful news, was incredible. Yes, he'd seen the article, so it wasn't actually a coincidence. But was this man *really* her friend's long-lost nephew? Somehow, it seemed just too pat and easy. Why didn't it ring true? Was it his manner she was reacting to, or the facts? And if he wasn't Anna's nephew, who *was* he?

She quickly asked God to help maintain her judgment, then reminded herself to give others the benefit of the doubt. Still . . . someone had to ask. After all, God keeps life mysterious, but that doesn't mean you should stop trying to figure it out, does it? "I'm afraid I don't understand," Gracie finally said. "Why did you never try to find your aunt and uncle before now?"

Tom shifted uncomfortably. "I . . . I wanted to but . . . well, my dad passed away a couple of years after my mom. Gram and Pop—uh, my grandparents—they hardly mentioned my parents, much less you guys. For a while, I didn't even think, but lately . . ."

"I understand," Anna replied, softly. "The need for family always comes back. For some folks, it just takes longer."

Tom nodded. "Do . . . do you think I could have a drink of water?"

"Of course!" Anna exclaimed. "Joe, dear, where are our manners? Gracie's brought us the loveliest scones, Tommy. You must be hungry."

"Sounds delicious. I am starved," Tom replied.

"Come with me," Joe said. The two men headed for the kitchen.

"Isn't he wonderful?" Anna asked, her face alight with pleasure.

"Yes," Gracie replied though she wasn't sure.

"There's an album," Anna said, gesturing toward a high-boy. Gracie rose and picked up the large book of well-thumbed photographs. "We don't have many pictures taken during those times. Can you see the ones Joe marked?"

There were several. One was a small, black and white group photo, two couples and one boy, all smiling. Gracie thought she recognized Anna and Joe. The photographs must have been taken over thirty years earlier. The other couple had to be her sister and brother-in-law. She peered at the boy's face. All she could make out was a shock of blond hair and a gap-toothed grin. The others were individual shots of the boy: swinging a bat, riding a bike, doing a handstand. His face wasn't much clearer in any of them.

"I don't have to see them," Anna said. "I know he's Connie's boy. Poor thing, he's been on his own these many years." Anna clasped her hands against her bosom. "It's all part of God's plan, don't you see? First, He blesses us with the reprinting of the books, and *because* of that, we've been reunited with our nephew."

She stared into space, eyes slightly uplifted. "Good things come in threes. I wonder what His third blessing will be."

Gracie's mind was too jumbled to think.

"Y OU WANT TO TELL ME why you seem so skeptical?"
Uncle Miltie asked, fastening his seatbelt.

Over a quick reheat of leftover lamb, baby carrots and
broccoli florets followed by scones and coffee, Gracie had
started to tell him the whole story. She needed to. It made
the entire event more real, somehow. She was so distracted
that she had almost forgotten to make the walnut squares for
Marybeth Bower's baby shower for Phyllis that evening. As a
result, Gracie was a bit behind schedule. The squares were
too hot to ice so she packed up the caramel-fudge frosting to
be applied later.

They were still discussing the Searfosses' remarkable news
as she put Fannie Mae in gear and took her foot off the brake.
She was dropping her uncle off at the seniors center for a

game or two of Scrabble before going onto Marybeth's. "I honestly don't know what to say. I kept feeling that I was in the middle of a movie, or a dream." She looked left, then right, then left again and pulled the dark-blue Cadillac out of her drive. "Of one thing, I am certain. Anna believes him."

"Gracie," Uncle Miltie looked troubled. "My question is, why don't *you*?"

Gracie turned the corner and headed downtown. "My dear Uncle Watson," she replied. "Sherlock Holmes may not have trusted his intution, preferring deduction. But I'm just Gracie Parks and, I don't know, I *just* have this feeling. . . ."

Uncle Miltie shifted in his seat, hands carefully holding the platter containing walnut squares. "These sure smell good. You going to serve these at the memorial set-up, too?" Both were relieved at the momentary change of subject.

Gracie nodded. "The icing's an experiment. If the ladies like it tonight, maybe I'll give it a go."

Uncle Miltie inhaled again. "Almost worth spending time with a bunch of women yattering on about babies . . . "

Gracie shot him a surprised glance.

Uncle Miltie grinned. "Just kidding. You know, that nephew coming home reminds me of some of the strange stories from the war."

Gracie remained silent. Her uncle didn't often speak of his war experiences, almost never about those as a POW. When he did, she wanted him to feel comfortable and under no pressure.

"You know, lots of men went missing. It was terrible. Their families were desperate." His eyes stared straight ahead. "I've heard tales of injured British soldiers returning home, and, even though they seemed very different from the way they'd been before, no one suspected things weren't on the up and up. I imagine, the folks kept telling themselves that it was the war that changed them. You can imagine how much they wanted to believe their son or husband was alive." Gracie nodded and slowed for a red light. "Sometimes, it took days, sometimes *months*, to discover that they were impostors." He shook his head. "A lot of the time, the families didn't really want to know. Can't say as I blame them."

They rode silently for a few blocks then Uncle Miltie asked, "What kind of conversation did you have with him?"

Gracie grimaced. "I'm not sure. I tried to pump him a little when Joe and Anna were out of the room, but he was pretty vague. He kept saying that he didn't remember much, that things were coming back in fits and starts. He asked questions about both of them, though."

"Sounds reasonable," her uncle replied. "After all, it's been years."

Gracie pulled into the parking lot. "I know. It's just that . . . the little things about him don't seem right. I can't quite put my finger on it. He's hiding something . . . I feel sure."

"You know what, my dear? The only real mystery may be why it took such charming books as Anna's so long to see the light of day again," he said, slowly getting out of the car.

O H, HE'S SO CUTE, I almost wish I had another one,"
Comfort Harding said, tickling Darren Michael under
the chin.

A group of the ladies of Willow Bend were gathered at
Marybeth and Herb Bower's bungalow to celebrate the
arrival of the Nickolsons' new baby. Most of the sandwiches,
relish trays and coffee had been consumed and all the gifts
unwrapped. As a result, Marybeth's rectangular living room
was a jumble of brightly colored wrapping paper, soiled
plates, hand-knitted infant wear and a variety of stuffed baby
toys. Gracie smiled at the star attraction who, after crying for
much of the evening, now gurgled quietly in his mother's
arms. She enjoyed these get-togethers, exchanging news and
recipes, and getting a chance to know better some of the
younger women in town, like Rick Harding's pretty wife. In

addition, she couldn't have found a tougher audience for her new icing.

"I'd have thought," Marge started, then swallowed the rest of a walnut square before finishing.

"*Umm*, this is *really* good, Gracie. Caramel-fudge, huh? Something else?"

"Sour cream," sugested Estelle Livett, a soprano and one of the few trained singers in the Eternal Hope choir— something she never let the other members forget.

"That'd be my guess," Nancy Bixler added.

Gracie smiled as Marge continued, "I'd have thought, Comfort, what with your daughter into her terrible twos, another baby would be the *last* thing you'd want."

Gracie had hoped that Rick's wife would join him in the choir. But so far, the young African-American mother had declined, preferring to sit in the lower pews with their daughter and listen to her husband's soaring tenor voice.

Estelle nodded, wiping her lips of errant caramel-fudge icing.

"I know," Comfort replied. "We're not planning another so soon, but," she looked wistful, "both Rick and I *love* children. There's nothing like a new baby, don't you think?"

"Amen," Gracie said. "Nothing like it in the world."

"I'll second that," Barb Jennings added, starting to pick up the wrapping paper. The director of the Eternal Hope choir never sat still for very long. It was this nervous energy that drove the choir, sometimes to lofty heights, sometimes just plain crazy. Several other ladies followed her lead, placing the toys and clothes into a couple of boxes.

"Another sandwich?" Marybeth asked, passing around an oval platter.

"No," Tish Ball started, interrupting her examination of a large illustrated picture book of *Jack and the Beanstalk*.

"Thank you," Tyne Anderson, her identical twin, finished. Although not musically gifted, the "Turner Twins," as they were known, could pull off a tune with the choir if they were seated side by side. And given plenty of time to rehearse. "But I wouldn't say no to another . . ."

"Of Gracie's delicious walnut squares," her sister completed the thought, reaching for the dessert tray.

"I'm making more coffee," Marybeth interjected. "Any takers?"

A chorus of voices sang yes.

"I'll give you a hand." Linda Cantrell, the high school librarian, rose, brushing crumbs from her skirt.

"Understand there was a fire outside Barry's Barber Shop," Comfort said. "Rick heard all about it while getting a trim."

"Uh huh," Tish replied. "John, too."

"And Bill," Tyne added. "But it was small and quickly put out."

"Who's put out?" Marybeth asked, re-entering the room. "Sorry to interrupt, but I forgot. Anyone for tea?"

"I'd love a cup. Thank you," Gracie said. "Oh . . . before I forget, I just wanted to remind you all of the war veterans' commemorative exhibit next Tuesday evening at six-thirty. Uncle Miltie and a bunch of his pals at the seniors center are keen to honor their efforts in the war. I'm hoping some of you will come and celebrate with them, after they've set it all up."

"We're catering," Marge added, with a wave of her arm. A chorus of metal bracelets tinkled. "Scrumptious desserts, of course. Can't tell you more than that, it's a secret. And you can dress the part, if you'd like. I'm dying to wear an old sweater and skirt set I've had for years."

"Count me in," Barb said. "Us, too," the twins chimed in.

"It's an open invitation," Gracie added. "Bring your families."

Estelle turned to Anna Searfoss, who was sitting quietly in a corner, her fingers gently stroking a finely crocheted, baby-blue infant nightshirt. "Speaking of family, I understand you've got even *more* good news, Anna."

"What?" Tish asked.

"Beyond the books being reprinted?" Tyne added.

Anna smiled softly. "Oh, yes! I've been ever so lucky, haven't I, Gracie?" Gracie touched her friend's hand. "My nephew, Tommy Williams, has returned to us. We'd given up hope of ever seeing him again. He's my sister's son, you understand. She died when he was just a boy—" a couple of women *tsked, tsked* in sympathy—"and, well it's a long story, but he was raised by his grandparents and, unfortunately, they never kept in touch."

"How'd he find you?" Marybeth asked. She was picking up stray bits of ribbon.

"That's the miracle," Anna said. "My books. He saw an article about the Lazy Lake reissues, recognized my photograph, got the number and gave us a call. Right out of the blue!"

"Probably used the Internet," Comfort said. "There isn't a night that Rick doesn't come home with some amazing tale of what's available on the worldwide Web."

"I hear that it's filled with all kinds of stuff that *shouldn't* be seen," Estelle said, her voice dripping with disapproval.

Comfort nodded.

"Oh, the *Internet*," Linda Cantrell's voice carried in from the kitchen. She stepped into the room carrying two mugs of coffee. "It used to terrify me, but now that it's in the school library, I've had a chance to surf a bit." She smiled ruefully. "Don't know what all the fuss's about. It took forever, and then the computer crashed. I gave up. Of course, Amy loves it. I'd rather she just stick to singing in the choir, much easier to keep track of her, but . . ." She handed a mug to Estelle and then gently wrapped one of Anna's hands around the other. "I try to keep an eye on what she's seeing when surfing the Net, but she's seventeen now, you know. You can't watch over their shoulders every minute."

"I'm worried about Katie," Phyllis said, stroking Darren's

back. "I hear horrible stories about what's available on the Internet . . . sometimes, it frightens the daylights out of me."

"I used to feel the same way but I've had a demonstration or two with Rick." It was Gracie's turn. "I think the devil you know's better than the devil you don't. "

The other ladies nodded.

"What'd you suggest?" Barb asked, folding crêpe paper.

"Well," Gracie replied, tasting another walnut square. *Not bad. A little too sweet?* She'd rethink the brown sugar and sour cream amounts if she made them for the seniors center. "It seems to me that we should take the bull by the horns. Organize some lessons for the older generations. Linda, do you know if the Internet's available in the public library, too?"

The school librarian nodded.

"That means it's accessible to all. Any chance we could arrange some lessons?"

"What a good idea!" Comfort said. "I'm sure Rick and some of his co-workers would be happy to volunteer as instructors. Shall I ask?"

Gracie looked at Linda, who smiled and said, "I'll give my counterpart a call. Might even find a few students willing to help. If you could get Rick to give me a call, perhaps, we can set up a schedule . . ."

Her head twisted in Gracie's direction. "What about advertising? How're we going to tell folks about it?"

"We could put it in the Sunday bulletins," Gracie replied. "That'll cover a lot of people to start."

"Uncle Miltie could put up a notice at the seniors center," Marge suggested.

Gracie nodded. "Then, if we don't get many takers, I guess I could ask Rocky. Maybe he'll let us put in a little ad in the *Gazette*."

"Offer him a plate of these walnut squares," Marge said, snatching the last one. "That man'll give you the whole front page."

PEOPLE!" BARB JENNING'S voice rang out in the choir loft of Eternal Hope Community Church. "Please. I know it's unusually hot, but can we try and *concentrate* a little?"

"We are—" Tish Ball began.

"Concentrating," Tyne finished their communal thought. "It's just that we—"

"Don't really like the *complicated* ones," Tish said, returning the favor.

Marge Lawrence fanned her face with sheet music and dropped into a nearby pew. Don Delano, a chemistry teacher at the local high school, wiped his wire-rimmed glasses, then joined her. Marybeth followed suit.

"Complicated," Estelle Livett snapped, a little moisture beading on her wrinkled brow. "You call *this* little hymn complicated?" She pulled herself upright. "I was just going to suggest that we give 'Oh Glorious King!' a chance. Any choir worth its salt has it in its repertoire. I used to sing it in my semi-professional days." She beamed to the rest of the choir. "We always had huge crowds. Mostly to hear me, of course."

Lester Twomley groaned, then coughed to cover it up. Don and Marge hid their faces behind their music sheets.

Gracie sighed. It was going to be a long afternoon. She dearly loved her choir friends and nothing gave her greater joy than to sing God's praise, but she disliked petty bickering, especially in His house. She wanted to say so, but in deference to Barb's position as choir director, she waited.

Instead of taking charge, Barb had lowered her eyes and begun to tap the baton nervously against her organ. Gracie knew she didn't handle criticism very well. But then, who did?

Don's baritone boomed from the pew. "Hope I'm not speaking out of turn, but I understood from the last two practices that we'd made our music selections for this term."

"Right on," Lester squeaked. "Been there. Done that. Bought the music . . . " he hesitated as the loft had gone completely silent. "So to speak," he finished lamely.

Barb nodded. Gracie jumped in for support. "The decision was made. Perhaps Estelle, we can put down the 'Oh Glorious King!' as a suggestion for next term?" Barb shot her a relieved smile.

"Is it complicated?" the blond twins asked simultaneously. Fortunately, as altos, they rarely had to carry the main melody.

"It's challenging, yes," Barb replied. "But, with little practice, not above our voices."

"Well, with summer coming, many members will be absent," Estelle continued. "We're already missing quite a few."

"Speaking of which . . . anybody know where Rick is?" Lester asked.

"He called," Barb replied. "Some sort of hardware crash. Sounded ominous."

"As I was saying," Estelle re-entered the conversation, "we're going to be short of a few voices. Especially sopranos. Amy's off to music camp, isn't she?" As their youngest member had been needed at her part-time job at Abe's Deli, Barb nodded in reply on her behalf. "It's an ideal time to try some new selections. I know of several songs with lovely solo parts."

"I'll bet you do," Lester whispered, standing behind Gracie.

"How about we get back to 'O For A Thousand Tongues,'" Marge said, checking her watch, "and discuss this at a later date?"

Don, Marybeth and Marge rose in unison and returned to their places. Barb grabbed the momentum, tapped her baton and began playing the introductory staves. Everyone picked up their music. The sopranos began to sing, "O for a thousand tongues to sing my great Redeemer's praise, the glories of my God and King, the triumphs of His Grace." Then, the altos and the tenors followed. Finally, Don's sole baritone rode the wave of the powerful chorus as it reached a crescendo. Gracie smiled while embracing the vigor of the old hymn with her own strong alto.

Lester began coughing.

Estelle tossed him an angry look.

Lester's face turned bright red, and he nearly tripped as he stepped out from behind his shared music stand. With an apologetic wave, he skipped down the stairs, coughing intermittently.

The choir regained their attention and continued for a couple of minutes.

"Fire! Help!" Lester's voice shouted, suddenly, over the sound of their voices.

Barb stopped playing and the choir stopped singing. "Did he say 'fire'?" Marge asked.

Don nodded, moving quickly. "Come on. We'd better go see."

They stumbled around the organ and thundered down the stairs. As the choir members marched along the aisle and out into the sunlight, Lester's cries continued.

"What's going on?" Don demanded as he descended the steps two at a time.

"Over here!" Lester's voice shouted. "Aoow! Give me a hand."

They trooped around the building, following his tenor voice. Don broke into a sprint.

When Gracie rounded the corner a few seconds later, she saw Don and Lester, sweat pouring off their faces, pulling on something with all their might.

A wave of heat overwhelmed her. Up against the side of the church stood a large trash can. Flames ten feet high danced in the air, lashing the church's wall.

A lot happened in the seven minutes it took for the Willow Bend Volunteer Fire Department Pumper Number One, lights and sirens on full blast, to rocket around the corner and burst into the parking lot, followed by Rick Harding in his van.

Lester and Don had stripped off their shirts and, using them as protective mittens, managed to drag the burning can away from the building. Unfortunately, the can tipped once and a tongue of fire greedily licked the dry grass and began racing across the lawn. With Gracie in charge and at the tap, the rest of the group had quickly formed a line from the fire to the kitchen and began passing jugs and bowls of water which Don and Lester took turns tossing into the blaze.

As the firefighters unreeled their hoses and began drenching the trash can, front lawn and the scorched side of the church, Rick Harding lugged out his medical kit and began examining Don and Lester's singed hands. The rest of the choir members collapsed on the front lawn, legs wobbly from exertion and throats raw from smoke.

"I haven't run that much," Tish sputtered. "Since I was a girl," said Tyne. Gracie, Marge and Barb burst out laughing.

Though it was difficult to tell from their outfits of hard hats and yellow-striped firefighters' clothes, Gracie thought she recognized Mike Struthers and Ben Tomlinson from the local newspaper, the *Mason County Gazette*, struggling at the end of a powerful hose. Too powerful, in fact, as the trash can shot backwards from the water's thrust, banging against the church. Herb Bower, whose cruiser had arrived a minute after the pumper, looked on from a respectful distance.

After the volunteers had extinguished both blazes within five minutes, they quickly began the clean-up.

Just as the excitement waned, Pastor Paul Meyer rounded the corner on his bike, knees pumping furiously. The choir members found their voices and legs and, simultaneously, began standing, stretching and competing to fill him in.

Gracie massaged her fingers and approached Don and Lester, each now dwarfed under an oversized firefighter's jacket. Mindful of their wrapped hands, she gave them each a kiss on the cheek and a gentle hug. "You were wonderful!" She glanced at Rick, who was packing up his medical kit. "Are they all right?"

"Both fine," the computer expert and part-time emergency medical technician said. "Lester's burns are a bit more serious, but he'll be okay in a week or so. Thank heavens you guys thought to use your shirts as hand protection." He shook his head, staring at the blackened church wall and patch of burnt, soggy lawn. "It could've been a lot worse." Rick clapped both men on the shoulder. "Sorry, guys, but I've got a sick hard drive to attend to."

Bike helmet in hand, a stunned Pastor Paul trotted over to join them. He clapped Lester and Don on the back, then nodded gratefully to Rick. "Thank heavens you acted quickly." He stared at the scorched side of the church, his expression one of disbelief. "I can't believe it! Who would have done such a thing? To a church! Our church! Can you imagine what would have happened if you weren't here? Oh, I don't even like to think . . ." The young minister paused, his face flushed. "I've only been gone an hour. It's a fluke that I've returned this quickly. I was visiting our newest member of the congregation, the Nickolsons' baby, but . . ." The flush on his face deepened. "The little tyke was feeding, so I went for a spin with Katie. What a chatterbox that little girl is! She nearly wore me out."

He was interrupted by the rest of the choir who trooped over to check on the two heroes. Rick looked at Lester. "Oh, almost forgot. That's going to start throbbing, if it hasn't already. Have you got any pain medication?"

Lester nodded, his eyes shockingly bright beneath his sooty face.

"Right," said Rick. "If it gets unbearable, head straight to the emergency room. Otherwise, I suggest you both visit your doctors tomorrow and get those dressings changed."

Gracie watched Rick's van roll down the street, then turned and waved good-bye to Marge and Barb. The two *Gazette* staffers approached, and took turns congratulating Don and Lester.

Gracie and Paul backed away, both running smack into Herb Bower. "Oh! Sorry, Herb," they exclaimed simultaneously

"It's all right," Herb replied. "Wasn't paying attention myself."

The trio began walking toward the parking lot.

"I'm surprised to see you here!" Gracie told the somber policeman. "This is an awfully small fire to warrant the chief of police's attention."

"Is there something we should know?" Pastor Paul asked.

Herb hesitated, his large body suddenly still. "Happened to be passing by, that's all."

They walked quietly. An idea slipped into Gracie's mind. "Herb, do you think the fire was deliberately set?"

"Dear Lord, no!" Paul exclaimed.

"What makes you ask that?"

Gracie shrugged but noticed something flicker in the police chief's eyes. "You *do*, don't you? You think it was arson. Is that what happened at Barry's?"

"Hold on," the pastor interrupted. "What happened at Barry's?"

Herb flipped up a large palm. "Now, wait a minute, Gracie." He glanced quickly around. The rest of the choir had left and the two firefighters were climbing aboard the pumper. "Don't jump to conclusions. I never said anything about Barry's or about arson."

"Very true," Gracie replied. "But your face tells a different story."

"I don't understand," Paul said. "Has this happened before? I'm the pastor of this church, Herb. I've a right to know."

Herb watched them for a moment, as though making a decision. He opened the door to Gracie's car. "Just pranks, that's all. Nothing for either of you to worry about." He waited until Gracie reluctantly got in, closed the door for her then strode toward the trash can, head bowed in thought, hands thrust deep into his pockets.

The minister leaned on her window. "Mind telling me what *that* was all about?"

Gracie shrugged. "Maybe nothing, Paul. Seems there was a minor fire at the barber shop." She tapped the steering wheel. "Could be just a coincidence."

The minister pursed his lips. "Well, it doesn't really matter, I guess." His eyes roamed over the soggy mess that used to be the Eternal Hope's front and side lawns. "I've got enough to worry about." He slapped the roof. "Better get to it. I'll see you, Gracie."

As Gracie started up Fannie Mae, she couldn't help wondering if this second fire had been a coincidence. Then she noticed the sun reflecting off the church's roof and shook her head. Reading more into the situation than was warranted, as usual. Gracie Parks, aka Miss Jane Marple. *Dear Lord*, she prayed to herself, *help me to be less suspicious and to accept Your creations at face value. Help me look for the bright side. To always look for the bright side. Amen.*

As the dark blue Caddy rolled onto the street, Gracie felt a little better.

AFTER EATING DINNER and doing the dishes, Gracie's unease slowly returned. Over dessert, Uncle Miltie had tried to convince her that arson wasn't the only option. "After all, dear," he'd said, returning the dish towel to the rack, "sometimes even coincidences aren't what they seem." Though she knew this was often true, she was still unconvinced, and left him staring intently at a ball game. Somehow, at the moment, watching grown men chase a small ball around a diamond seemed awfully foolish and unimportant. Gracie couldn't get past the thought that someone had deliberately started a fire and almost condemned her church, herself and her precious friends to a deadly conflagration. *Why would anyone do such a wicked thing?*

Needing some air, she called to Gooseberry and they headed out for a walk. A little time to think, to be close to her natural surroundings, to believe that her community was safe. She marched rapidly down her street, waving to the Griswolds who were sitting on their front porch. Gooseberry happily scooted ahead, dashing into hedges, disappearing for several seconds then reappearing just in front of her. She chuckled as his orange tummy squirmed through a particularly tight knot of branches.

Inhaling the lovely scent of late spring and enjoying the greetings of passersby, Gracie's spirits quickly rose. Thanking God for her safety, she silently recited a favorite passage from the Book of Acts: "Thou hast made known to me the ways of life: Thou shalt make me full of joy with Thy countenance."

It was only when Gooseberry darted around a heavily treed corner that Gracie realized she was approaching the Searfosses'. Funny how the unconscious directs us. *"Or is it You?"* she pondered, eyes upward.

Gooseberry hissed. Startled, she glanced down to find her tomcat's fur and tail standing on end. Her nose wrinkled. *Smoke!*

Just as she yelled "fire!" the front door of the Searfoss house burst open and Tom Williams leapt down the front steps, trailed by fingers of dark smoke. Almost knocking her flat, he sprinted across the lawn and up the street. Staring after him for a split second, Gracie then gathered her wits and raced up the stairs shouting her friends' names.

The hallway was thick with smoke. Flames were licking

the drapery around a window frame. Dropping to her knees, Gracie crawled toward the living room while still hollering for her friends. She could barely see, and the blanket of heat almost overpowered her.

"Help!" a man's voice bellowed. "Please, help us!"

"Joe! It's Gracie. Hang on, Joe. Hang on!" She pounded on the wall. "I'm coming. Where are you?"

"Living room. Hurry!"

Feeling the door opening with her hands, Gracie ignored the burning in her eyes and called to Joe. He yelled again. She followed his voice through the gloom until his hand snaked onto her arm. She felt Anna fingers gripping her shoulder. Her friend was coughing violently. Gracie almost wept with relief when she heard the distant whine of a fire truck. "It's okay," she said, struggling with Joe to pull Anna to her feet. "Help's on the way."

Together, the three lurched into and down the hallway. Struggling with Anna's weight, Gracie bumped into the wall and bit back a scream. Her arm felt like it was on fire.

Tom, now mysteriously returned to the doorstep, lifted his aunt into his arms. She seemed limp and small in his grasp. A fire truck wailed around the corner and screeched to a halt in the driveway. Once again, uniformed men jumped off and began hauling heavy black hoses.

As Gracie and Joe stumbled into the evening light, Tom carried Anna down the steps and laid her gently on the grass.

A firefighter ran over and asked if there was anyone else inside. Tears streaming down his lined face, Joe Searfoss shook his head and then began to cough explosively. A roar filled Gracie's head as water exploded from the hoses, streaming toward the flames which now stretched well into the sky.

Gracie felt a hand on her good arm. She turned to find Rick Harding with an oxygen mask in his hand.

"This just isn't your lucky day," he said, his dark face concerned.

She glanced down and saw another medical technician ministering to the Searfosses. Rick helped Gracie to sit on the grass, then strapped the mask over her head. Gently, he applied ointment to her burnt arm.

Gracie Parks inhaled deeply, giving thanks with every breath.

Nothing had ever tasted so sweet!

10

PART OF THE SEARFOSS house seemed to burn like a roman candle. Struggling valiantly, the Willow Bend Volunteer Fire Department contained the skyrocketing flames. The second pumper slid to a halt on the lawn and its firefighters quickly began wetting the houses nearby. The emergency lights from the firetrucks and police cruisers throbbed, casting the neighborhood in a garish red glow.

Anna was in shock. Oxygen mask still hugging her face, the elderly woman clung to her equally stunned husband as he and Rick moved her gently into the back of Herb Bower's cruiser. An ambulance from Keefer Memorial was on its way, they were told.

Gracie felt nauseous, her skin alternating between prickling heat and chilling goosebumps. Removing the mask, she took her first hesitant breath of the charcoal thick air surrounding the inferno. Her throat was as raw as if she had swallowed smoldering ashes. She spied Tom Williams on the sidewalk, his arms gesturing wildly, as he spoke with the police chief. A crowd had gathered, and Officer Jim Thompson was loudly encouraging people to move back. Sue Jameson, the features editor from the *Mason County Gazette*, was rushing about, interviewing anyone willing to talk. One thought, however, burned more brightly in Gracie's mind than the last tongues of flame licking the darkening sky: why had Tom Williams run from the burning house?

She swallowed, took a deep draught of oxygen and marched over, ignoring the fascinated throng. Without pre-amble, Gracie demanded in a hoarse whisper, "Tom, why weren't you trying to save your aunt and uncle? I saw you run out past me!"

He blinked, his face glowing with sweat. "What?" His mouth opened and shut like a landed fish. "I . . . well, I smelled smoke and ran for help." He gestured toward the fire trucks.

"You didn't go in? You didn't *bother* to check and see if Anna and Joe were *trapped* inside? How could you? They . . . oh, dear God, they could have died."

Tom flushed darkly and tightly shut his mouth. Eyes shaded by the brim of his hat, Herb Bower eyed them with interest.

Arms akimbo, Gracie stared up at Tom, waiting.

Finally, it all came out in a mumbled rush. "I . . . guess I . . . I panicked. I . . . opened the door and . . . I just didn't *think*." Tom sputtered. "You've got to believe me, Mrs. Parks! I'd never do them any harm. They're my only relatives. *Please*, you've got to believe me."

"Gracie!" a familiar voice boomed from a knot of onlookers.

She turned to see Marge and Uncle Miltie shoving past Officer Thompson.

Marge reached her first and enveloped her friend in a powerful hug. Uncle Miltie's eyes were damp as he clutched his niece's hands in his own. "My dear, thank the good Lord you're safe." He squeezed her hands tightly. "We heard all about it. Do you know you're a hero!"

It was only then, surrounded by the protection and love of her uncle and friend, that Gracie realized the extent of the risk she had taken. She began to shake uncontrollably and tears streamed down her stained face. Uncle Miltie slipped his coat over her shoulders and Marge shielded her from prying eyes.

"I need to speak to you," Herb Bower said, tugging loose a small notepad.

"Can't it wait?" Marge asked. "She's been through an awful lot."

The police chief hesitated, then shoved the pad back into his breast pocket. "Yeah. Get some rest, Gracie. You sure were in the right place today." He tipped his hat. "I'll touch base with you later. You really were a godsend!" He shook his head wonderingly.

"Let's go home," her uncle whispered.

Gracie nodded, but then she noticed Tom and Rick approaching the police cruiser in which Joe and Anna still huddled.

"Just one moment," she said to Uncle Miltie. She arrived at the sedan just as Tom was inviting his relatives to join him at Cordelia Fountain's Tourist Home.

"There's an ambulance on the way. I really think they should go to the hospital," Rick was saying.

In tears, Anna shook her head. "No, Joe," her voice rasped. "I don't want the hospital, please."

Gracie glanced at Rick. "Is hospitalization necessary?"

He shrugged. "Just a precaution. They both seem fine, but some observation wouldn't hurt. It's what I'd recommend, for sure."

"I'm sure you're right. But, even knowing that, I think they'd be more comfortable at my place," she said, reaching in to touch Anna's shoulder. "Why don't you and Joe come and stay with Uncle Miltie and me? We'd love to have you."

Anna smiled hesitantly. "We don't have any clothes . . . anything." Her smile faded. "Oh, dear! I'll have to get some insulin."

"Don't worry, honey," her husband replied. "I'll take care of that."

"We'll make you comfortable, Anna. Don't worry," Uncle Miltie reassured her.

Anna sighed. "I guess it will be a little while before we can go back home, Joe?"

At the moment, before them was a charred and smoldering structure. Tears glistening in his deep-set eyes, Joe glanced at Gracie and shook his head, as if to say: *She doesn't know the extent of the damage.* "Yes, dear," he answered softly. "It may be a little while."

11

ARLY FRIDAY MORNING, the sun shone brilliantly, bathing Willow Bend in a golden light. As Gracie returned, wonderfully invigorated from her walk, she found yesterday's disastrous events difficult to believe. She was still almost intoxicated, or at least giddy from her brush with danger, yet thrilled and thankful that she had risen to the occasion. She almost couldn't believe that she'd gone into the burning house without hesitation. She knew that her daring was due to heavenly courage. It would take a while, she recognized, before she really could accept what had happened. Though she'd been called a hero, she found that designation daunting and inaccurate. After all, she had been guided by a higher power.

Stroking Gooseberry's back, she considered the circumstances of the two fires back to back. Three, actually, when she added the incident at Barry's Barber Shop. Gooseberry's white paws grasped at a long blade of grass. Just coincidence, she reminded herself, tickling his tummy when he rolled over. Fires must happen all the time, even in a small sleepy town like Willow Bend.

Gracie eyed her own house with its wide porch, large rhododendrons and split-rail fence. She knew she was very fortunate. She and Elmo had been very happy there, raising Arlen, and being active in the community they both loved so well. On the surface, though her throat felt a little scratchy, life still seemed wonderful. The burn on her arm was already healing. It was only when she heard Anna and Joe's voices in the kitchen that her illusion of a perfect world became one she could no longer hold on to. Her dear friends' cherished home was damaged, some of their precious belongings were destroyed. And they had almost lost their lives. *Thank You, dear Lord, for using me to accomplish Your work and for blessing me with the opportunity and the strength to save my friends. I am forever under Your sacred wing.*

Gracie pulled open the screen door and stepped in. Gooseberry streaked through her legs and made a beeline for his dish. "Good morning, all." She walked around the table and gave Anna's shoulders a quick squeeze. Her friend's face was haggard, dark smudges already underlining her eyes. Joe stood and they hugged briefly.

"I'm sorry I wasn't here to greet you when you woke. I

thought you'd both be exhausted and need extra sleep." She cocked an eye towards Anna. Joe nodded. *So he told her. Poor Anna. It'll be a while before their home is inhabitable. And, it'll never be the same.*

"We've only just gotten up," Joe said, his voice slightly hoarse from smoke exposure. He took his wife's hand. "We don't know how to thank you, Gracie," he said, swallowing hard. "You saved our lives."

"Dear Gracie, you were wonderful!" Anna added softly. "I wouldn't have made it without you." She reached for Gracie's hand. "You'll be in our prayers, always."

Gracie blushed slightly and squeezed Anna's frail fingers. "I'm just grateful that the dear Lord allowed me to help. Now, I see Uncle Miltie was going to start breakfast?"

"Me?" Uncle Miltie squeaked.

Joe laughed. Anna forced a chuckle.

Gracie smiled. It was good to see her friends laugh, if only a little.

"How does a broccoli and cheese omelet, with hash browns and sourdough bread, sound?"

"Like the Angel Gabriel singing the Lord's praises," Joe said.

"Amen," Uncle Miltie added.

"Would that be all right for you, Anna?" Gracie sensed the anxiety lurking below the surface of their conversations. Everyone was trying hard to be upbeat.

"That would be fine," Anna said, her voice barely above a whisper.

Gracie began gathering ingredients as Uncle Miltie and Joe laid the table.

"It'll be fun, having you both here. We can try out a few new recipes," Gracie said, handing Joe a block of cheese to grate. She rummaged in the refrigerator for some cooked potatoes. Uncle Miltie began chopping them into cubes.

Offering his wife a piece of cheese, Joe paused. "My Anna's a great cook, as you know, yet somehow, she makes sure we eat a sensible diet. I'm sure, in no time, the two of you will have us letting out our waistbands."

They chatted over a leisurely breakfast, studiously avoiding any discussions on the fire. When they had finished, Uncle Miltie asked Joe to help him rearrange the downstairs furniture and remove the rugs, to make it easy for Anna to move around. Watching the men work, Gracie's anger from the day before returned. She was worried about Anna's health. Being caught in a fire was stressful enough for anyone, much less an elderly diabetic. Gracie couldn't help thinking that Tom Williams's sudden arrival, the declaration of his relationship to the Searfosses and his cowardly behavior during the fire were somehow connected to the tragedy at the Searfoss house.

After all, she imagined that the photo album with the pictures of young Tommy Williams must now be destroyed. Not that those old snapshots provided much proof of identity, but if they were the only photos of the Searfosses' nephew, they had just gone up in smoke. It was a bit too much of a coincidence. And recently, Gracie was being forced to accept too many of those.

Gracie's reverie was broken by Uncle Miltie. "I'm way too old for this," he declared, assisting Joe in carrying a coffee table to the wall. "The old body doesn't respond the way it used to."

Anna tapped her cane on the wooden floor. "I hear you moving about, George Morgan. You're not using your walker and you've got the step of a sixty-year-old."

"And the appetite of a teenager," Joe added, guiding his wife carefully around the various pieces of furniture. Gracie was impressed with Anna's ability to find humor in the face of such tragedy.

"We're going to be fine, aren't we, dear?" Joe asked his wife, as she slowly explored the room. Gooseberry silently followed her from a safe distance. Anna paused. "After all, it's only until we get the house fixed up," he added, heartily.

"Do you think He's done this on purpose?" Anna whispered, her face suddenly clouded with worry.

Surely she didn't suspect Tom, too? Startled, Gracie asked, "Who? Who's done what on purpose?"

"The Lord. He's given us so much and I . . . I was still waiting for his third blessing." Anna rubbed her hands. "Thou shalt not covet . . ."

"No!" Gracie and Joe interrupted simultaneously.

"It was an accident, darling," Joe said, turning and holding his wife.

"That's right," Gracie added, moving to Anna's side. "It was no one's fault. Sometimes bad things just happen. We don't always understand why. You know He works in mysterious ways."

"That's right," Joe repeated. "Just an accident. We've got insurance. It'll be fine."

"Of course," Anna replied softly, grasping Gracie's fingers. "Thank goodness."

Gracie squeezed her friend's hand. With the furniture rearranged and Uncle Miltie temporarily sleeping upstairs, Anna and Joe would be almost at home on the main floor. She would do her utmost to make them comfortable. Everything *was* going to be fine.

"If you ladies don't need us anymore," her uncle said, "Joe and I are going to sit for a spell on the front porch, review some of my war photos and toss around some ideas for the memorial display."

"Not sure if any of my memorabilia survived the fire," Joe added. "But I'd still like to play a part."

"Go ahead, dears," Anna said. "It'll do you good to have something to work on."

In a couple of minutes, Joe and Uncle Miltie were sipping coffee and rocking in the large front swing, chatting intensely over a loose pile of old black and white snapshots. Gracie poured Anna a cup of tea and excused herself momentarily. She nipped upstairs and, using an extension phone, began making the first of a number of calls to the members of the Willow Bend Town Council.

"Mayor Ritter," she said. In a moment, Tom Ritter's voice was in her ear.

"Gracie Parks! I was just going to call you, see if you're all right," he said. "Understand you're to be congratulated, a real heroine."

"Thank you, Tom," Gracie replied. "But I just happened to be in the right place at the right time, thanks to the good Lord."

"Maybe so, but you're mighty brave, Gracie. Why, I can even hear the smoke damage in your voice! Not sure too many folks would have done what you did. Ben Tomlinson says you charged into the Searfosses' without care or consideration of your own safety. I call that heroic! Sure hope I'd have been able to do the same in your shoes."

Gracie didn't know what to say. She honestly didn't feel that she had done anything other than act on instinct directed solely by divine guidance. That was all. So, she remained silent.

"Hear you've got Anna and Joe with you? How *are* they?"

"Shaken but fine, I think. No real physical injuries other than a bit of smoke inhalation, but emotionally, Tom . . . I really don't know. Anna's health is delicate. She loved her house, they've lived there for years. Uncle Miltie and I're doing our best to reduce her stress, get her to rest while the damage is fixed."

"Must have been a terrible experience for them! And now, having to temporarily move . . . the poor things. I can't imagine. Still, they're lucky to have friends like you and your uncle. It's mighty good of you to put them up, Gracie. Mighty good. You'll give them my regards, won't you? Sounds as if leaving them alone's the best thing to do."

"Very thoughtful, Tom. I'll let them know. In fact, Anna and Joe're the reason I'm calling. Before the disaster with the fire started, they received some grand news."

"Oh?"

"Did you know Anna was the author of a series of children's books?"

The mayor hesitated. "I think I heard something about that."

"Many years ago, she'd written a series about an Indiana family around the turn of the century. Well, now a large New York publishing house is planning to reprint those books."

"Wonderful!"

"I thought it would be nice if the town officially congratulated her. As our very own literary success."

"*Hmm.* A nice idea, Gracie. What do you have in mind?"

"Well, I haven't thought it totally through yet . . . I wanted input from you and some of the other councillors, but I was thinking that she could be honored at a small ceremony, perhaps even a surprise."

"Hey! I like that idea," the mayor replied. He paused. Gracie could almost hear the gears whirling in his head. "We could even turn something like this into an annual honor. Yeah! Each year, Willow Bend celebrates its homegrown stars! A surprise, huh? You mean, a surprise to the town or the honoree?"

"In Anna's case, I was thinking we would keep it a secret from her for a little while, until we had the plans ready."

"That might be interesting. What if it were a complete surprise?"

"I don't know," Gracie replied. "I tend to think that half of the fun is in the anticipation."

"You've got a point there, Gracie. Great expectations and all that. On the other hand, with only a select few knowing until the last minute . . . *hmm*, that has wonderful potential, too, Gracie. We can even ask the townfolk to offer suggestions for other possible honorees. *Hmm* . . . let me see." His voice rose in excitement. "Yeah. I can see it! Large crowds, a brass band playing, a ribbon-cutting ceremony, with me naturally, as mayor, giving Anna a key to the city. I like it! By gosh, Gracie, I like it a lot."

Gracie almost groaned. Like all politicians, Willow Bend's mayor could be startlingly quick to pounce on a positive political opportunity.

"Well," Gracie replied. "Something like that. As long as the focus is on honoring Anna Searfoss. I'd like her to know. But for the other years, well, when the time comes, we could try for a complete surprise. How about a planning committee? I'd be willing to volunteer."

"Another excellent suggestion. Wouldn't think of one without you. I'll offer it for discussion at the next council meeting. How's that?"

"That would be fine, thank you. I was planning to call the other councillors—"

"Won't be necessary, Gracie. I'll tell them. You just take good care of our literary celebrity, and don't forget to tell them that Tom Ritter sends his regards, okay?"

Gracie promised, then hung up.

She decided not to tell Anna and Joe anything yet. She knew that given the correct timing, the Searfosses would be thrilled to learn that they were to receive a tribute from their community.

Instinctively, Gracie Parks realized that, right now, though, there could be such a thing as one surprise too many.

12

THE PHONE WAS RINGING as Gracie re-entered the kitchen. Hurriedly, she picked it up, fearing that the mayor was calling her back. She didn't want either Joe or Anna to find out accidentally about her suggested celebration. "Hello?"

"Gracie! Are you all right?" The booming voice belonged to her old friend, Rocky Gravino, editor and owner of the lively *Mason County Gazette*. "Ben and Sue told me all about the fire. Full reports. You must be crazy, woman! Running into a burning building. You could have been killed."

"I'm fine," she replied simply.

"Thank heavens, but still, that was a very foolish thing to do!"

Gracie was growing a little weary of all the attention. "I only did what was necessary."

"Of course, you did, Gracie. I didn't mean . . . it's just that, well, I was worried about you."

Gracie smiled softly. It was nice to hear him say that.

"You *look* awful."

"Pardon?" she asked, startled. She heard a flutter from something sounding like thick paper.

"You should see the photograph Sue snapped of you. Good grief, woman! You're black with soot, head to toe, and your face's covered by an oxygen mask. You look like something from a grade-B horror film."

Gracie recalled a flash startling her outside the Searfoss house. "I hadn't realized that she'd taken a photo."

"Well, Ben was doing other duty. But you're set for the front page. Any chance we can get together so I can interview you for the story?"

Gracie sighed. The attention wasn't going to go away. "There's nothing I have to say, Rocky. I'm just thankful to God that Anna and Joe are safe."

"May I quote you?"

"If you must."

"Come on, Gracie! You're our hero of the hour, whether you like it or not. You saved Anna and Joe's lives and the folks of Willow Bend want to know all about it." He paused for a moment. "Uh, I guess I can't speak with Anna and Joe?"

"I don't think that'd be a good idea, Rocky. They're exhausted and Anna's very distressed. They both need to be left alone to heal."

"You're right, of course. Okay, I'll get Sue to do the story with what she's already got."

Ten minutes later the phone rang again.

A man's voice answered. "Mrs. Anna Searfoss, please."

Gracie put her hand over the receiver. "May I ask who's calling?"

"Name's Arnie Houston of the Houston Entertainment Agency. Well, I've got something of tremendous importance to discuss with Mrs. Searfoss. I got your phone number from the local newspaper office."

Gracie hesitated.

"If it's for me," Anna said, "it's all right."

"Just one moment, please," Gracie replied, handing the phone to her friend. While Anna began to talk, Gracie quickly and quietly cleared the table.

"Anna Searfoss speaking. Yes, I'm the author of the Lazy Lake series." Anna paused, listening. "You've read my books? How wonderful! I'm sorry, your name is?" Another pause. "Mr. Houston. Yes, well, thank you for telling me. Oh. You're a what? An agent?" Anna's forehead wrinkled. Gracie busied herself with tidying up, wondering if she should leave the room. "I'm sorry, I don't understand. My books are already being reprinted. I don't need representation." She swallowed hard. Gracie quickly gave her a glass of water.

Gracie heard the man's voice, suddenly pitched louder.

"You want to come to Willow Bend? Just a minute, please," Anna said, then covered the receiver with her palm. "It's an agent, Gracie. I'm a little confused, but he says he has a deal he wants to discuss with me. Sounds very exciting! Is it all right if he comes here?"

"Of course," Gracie replied.

Anna returned to the phone and gave the man Gracie's address. "Tomorrow afternoon. Yes, that would be fine. Yes, me too. Thank you, Mr. Houston." Anna placed the receiver on the hook and clapped her hands together.

"Who was that, dear?" Joe asked as he and Uncle Miltie entered the kitchen, their hands clutching photographs.

"Oh, Joe! It's very exciting. It was a Mr. Arnie Houston, from New York. An agent."

Joe sat beside his wife and plopped a pile of snapshots on the table. "Agent? What'd he want?"

Anna smiled brilliantly. "He loved my books. Says he saw the news story on them and has some sort of deal he wants to discuss with me. He's coming here tomorrow. Can you believe it?"

"That's very exciting, Anna," her husband replied. Uncle Miltie chimed in his agreement.

Gracie felt a flutter in her stomach, but she wasn't sure if it was from excitement or apprehension. Too many people

84

seemed interested in tracking down this one elderly woman. She saw the excited flush in Anna's face and scolded herself. *Stop second-guessing everything, Gracie Parks!*

"It's great news," she said finally. "And very much deserved."

13

THE NEXT AFTERNOON after a lunch of tuna and tomato sandwiches, Gracie filled the sink with soapy water while Joe started clearing the table. Anna had her dish towel ready for drying. Uncle Miltie was fiddling with the latch on the screen door and entertaining them with jokes. "Why do shoemakers go to heaven?" He paused. "Because they have good soles. Get it?" The others groaned. Uncle Miltie grinned and twisted the screwdriver.

"Please, Joe," Gracie said. "Sit and enjoy your coffee."

"And watch you work? No, thanks," he replied. "I can drink and clear at the same time."

"How about this one?" Uncle Miltie squirted some oil into the hinge. "A hungry lion was roaming through the jungle looking for something to eat. He came across two men. One was sitting under a tree and reading a book, and the other was typing away on his typewriter." He closed the screen door with a snap, wiped his hands on a rag then joined Anna at the table. "You're going to love this one, Anna," he said, touching her hand. "The lion quickly pounced on the man reading the book and devoured him." He waited a beat. "Even the king of the jungle knows that readers digest and writers cramp."

Anna laughed.

"Oh," sighed Joe. "That one's really—"

"No!" Gracie shouted out the window.

The sickening sounds of screeching tires followed by a child's cry filled the kitchen. "Oh dear!" Gracie exclaimed, already half out the screen door. As she and Joe raced down the steps, the stench of burning rubber bit into the afternoon air.

Her head safely enveloped in a neon-blue helmet, Katie Nickolson was sprawled on Gracie's lawn. The handle bars of her red bike were near the front wheel of a gleaming silver sedan, parked askew on the road. A young man with spiked blond hair, sunglasses and a cell phone stood glaring down at the wailing child. He whirled at the sound of their footsteps, a still-glowing cigarette dangling from his lip. "It's not my fault! She . . . she came out of nowhere!"

Gracie ignored him and ran to the child. "Katie! Don't move, honey. Are you all right?"

The girl stopped crying and nodded. "My bike!" She jumped to her feet. "Did he break my bike?"

"Your bike!" the stranger exploded. "I never touched your bike. What about my car?" He started dialing his cell phone.

"I hope you're calling the police," Gracie said as she examined the girl.

"That's right," Joe added, stepping alongside Gracie.

Though frightened, Katie's injuries seemed no more than a grass-stained knee and bruised pride. *Praise God*, Gracie thought.

"Police?" The young man snapped shut the phone. "Why, you can see she's perfectly okay. We don't need the police." He took a quick drag of the cigarette, then gave Katie a dazzling smile. "You're all right, aren't you, honey?"

"Don't call me that!" Katie snapped. "You're bad. You almost ran me over."

The man yanked off his sunglasses. "Me?! *You* jumped out from behind that car, little girl," he said, pointing to a van parked in front of Marge Lawrence's house.

"Did not," Katie said.

"Did so."

"Did not."

The young man opened his mouth, but Gracie stopped him with a raised hand.

"Did so," a new voice said.

They all turned. Marge Lawrence strolled casually across the grass as if she were the headliner for a fashion show. She approached Katie. "Now, honeybunch, I saw it from my window. You weren't paying attention, were you?"

The girl's face fell.

Marge gave her thin shoulders a squeeze. "You're a very lucky little girl. He stopped just in time. You just lost your balance, didn't you?"

The stranger grinned, dropped the cigarette on the sidewalk and stomped heavily. "Right on."

"And you!" Marge snapped. "We ought to call the police. Driving way too fast for a residential street."

By this time, Uncle Miltie had arrived at his niece's side. Anna stood on the porch, listening intently.

The man ran his fingers through his hair. It stood up more wildly than ever. Gracie guessed he was in his mid-twenties. "Listen, no harm done. Right?" He picked the bike up and rolled it to Katie. She yanked it from his hands, jumped on and began riding in circles. He looked at the knot of people on Gracie's lawn. Across the street, Mrs. Hadlock stared from her porch. Then he reached into his pocket, removed a roll of bills and plucked free a fifty. "This should cover any damages, right?"

Gracie watched Katie. She had to admit the girl certainly didn't seem any worse for wear. "You're sure she wasn't hit?" she asked Marge.

Her friend shook her head. "Got frightened and plopped over onto your lawn. She wasn't going very fast."

"Okay?" the man asked, waving the bill.

"I'll need to copy the information off of your driver's license, just in case. And you'll have to give the money directly to her parents and explain," Gracie replied.

He eyed the silent group, then exhaled and pushed the bill into his pocket. "Deal. Now, maybe you can do something for me," he added, his face brightening. He stuck out a beautifully manicured hand. "I'm Arnie Houston of the Houston Entertainment Agency. Any idea where I can find Anna Searfoss?"

14

DO YOU KNOW THAT CHILDREN'S entertainment is one of the fastest growing segments of the industry?" Arnie Houston asked fifteen minutes later as he quickly stalked back and forth in Gracie's living room. Gooseberry sprawled along the window ledge, his tail flicking sporadically.

Anna and Joe sat side by side on Gracie's couch, and Uncle Miltie lounged in the big arm chair near the window. Gracie stood in the entrance, a tray containing drinks and a plateful of cookies in her hands. The other armchair remained empty, as Arnie Houston refused to sit. Instead, he paced. Uncle Miltie had given up following the young man's movements, although Joe's eyes never left the tailored suit. Gracie felt as though an impeccably dressed whirlwind had touched down in the middle of her home. *Poor Joe!* she thought. *He's going to get a stiff neck.*

"Well, they are!" The stranger sneezed. His hand snaked into a pocket and pulled out a package of cigarettes. "Excuse me. It's amazing, but what works best are the kind of stories you wrote, Mrs. Searfoss."

"No smoking, thank you."

"What? Oh, sorry." As Houston's stride quickened, so did his speech. "I mean those that appeal both to kids and adults."

"Thank you, young man," Anna said, her face brightening. "But please, won't you sit down?"

Houston shook his head. "Too psyched up. Getting a chance to meet you is so special, my mind's on fast-forward."

"It's hard on our concentration, young man," Uncle Miltie joked, gesturing to the empty chair. "If you don't *sit down*, I'm going to start following you."

"All that movement must make you thirsty," Gracie added, moving forward and offering Houston a glass.

The young man blinked, then perched on the armchair. He took a gulp while Gracie handed the others a glass. Houston grimaced. "This is . . ."

"Homemade lemonade," Uncle Miltie replied, smacking his lips. He bit into a cookie. "Gracie's is the best. Try a molasses cookie."

Both Joe and Anna murmured their approval.

"Uh," Houston said, placing the drink on a side table as if the glass carried a disease. He glanced at the cookie and pursed his lips. "How 'bout a Perrier with a twist of lemon?"

"Perrier?" Uncle Miltie asked. "Isn't that just—"

"I'm sorry," Gracie said, interrupting. "I don't have any Perrier. Would you prefer coffee? I've just—"

Houston nodded. "Now you're talking. Double-short latte would be fab. And a couple of low-fat biscotti." He swivelled, turning his attention back to Anna. "Now, as I was saying, Mrs. Searfoss, there are these family-oriented television networks that're just—"

"Ahh . . . double-short . . . low-fat?" Gracie asked, glancing from Uncle Miltie and Joe. They both shrugged.

"Latte. Biscotti." He sneezed again. "Sorry. You've got biscotti in Willow Bend, right?" Gracie did not have a clue what a low-fat biscotti was, so she didn't say anything. Instead, she quietly sat down, across from her uncle. Houston motored on. "The cable networks, they're just dying for product. You see, they've got twenty-four hours a day to fill. They're overrun with cartoons and animal stuff. But . . . the tweens, they're real tough to program for. Now, something like your Lazy Lake stories—apple-pie family values, pioneering times—why, they're going to eat it up."

Gracie watched the faces of her friends. Joe looked dumfounded while Anna glowed.

A cell phone rang. Just as Gracie was rising to find hers, Houston ripped a tiny, gold-colored one off his belt and began yelling into it. Gooseberry leapt from the window and stalked into the kitchen. Gracie sank back into her chair. Uncle Miltie winked at her slowly.

"Yeah? Yeah, that's right. No . . . no, *exclusive*. No other way. Uh uh. I don't *do* non-exclusive. You tell your client: he wants to work with me, he does it my way. He'll see the light." He snapped the phone shut. "Sorry. Now, where was I? Oh, yeah." Houston reached into his jacket and pulled out a long folded sheet of paper. "This is your ticket, Mrs. Searfoss. Sign with me *today* for exclusive representation, and I guarantee you that millions of kids're gonna fall all over Scotty and Suzy." He hooted then sneezed. "Allergic to cats," he said. "That old-time setting, it's perfect! Back to the land. Back to the lake! A simpler life, that sort of stuff. A real easy pitch, you know: *Little House* meets *Bonanza*." He frowned. "Not quite right, but something like that."

"Oh," Anna replied. "We don't know anything about the business of television, do we, Joe?"

Her husband rubbed his neck. "We sure don't, we just watch it."

Houston flashed a megawatt smile and slapped the paper. "That's where *I* come in. Ask anybody, Mrs. Searfoss. *I'm* the man. It's my business . . . selling products to these guys. I'm very good. I do it *every* day. You've written—what?—ten books?" He licked his lips. "That's twenty half hours off the bat. But that's just the beginning. Then we're off to the races. Show'll be a guaranteed hit, no ifs, ands or buts. Probably be picked up for—who knows?—four or five seasons. Then SYN-DI-CA-TION!" he tossed his head back and crowed. "The bucks will really roll in."

Gracie had risen, scooped up a dozing Gooseberry, and popped him out the back door. She returned to her chair and sipped lemonade. *This young man was very good,* she thought. *Very good.* The question was, at what? Being an agent or a salesman? And why all the rush? She understood how easily Joe and Anna might be won over. After all, Houston's interest was very flattering, and a television series meant more exposure and more money. But as her dear Elmo had been fond of saying: *Look before you leap.* Arnie Houston may well be one of the best agents around. That didn't mean the Searfosses shouldn't be prudent. As their longtime friend, Gracie felt responsible for their welfare.

The young agent smiled again and reached for a pen from his breast pocket. He handed both contract and pen to Joe. "We'll have another *Waltons.* And the merchandising!" He paused, thinking. "All we need is your signature, Mrs. Searfoss, and the full services of the Houston Entertainment Agency are at your service." He leaned forward to pump Anna's hand. "They're going to *love* you, lady!" he said. "I already do."

"It's so exciting," Anna said. "I don't know what to say."

"Say yes," Houston replied. "You can't lose."

"What do you think, Joe?" she asked.

Her husband glanced down at the contract and eyed the expensive pen. "I don't know, darling. It sounds awfully good—"

"Course it does," Houston bragged, jumping up. "It's not like falling off a log to get a series on television, let me tell you. And *no one* has my contacts. No one. Of course," he paused dramtically. "It's only fair to tell you know that I'm considering signing a couple of other properties. Who knows? If they sign more quickly, the networks' fall schedules could be all wrapped up. Your Lazy Lake family could be left high and dry. We wouldn't want that, now would we?"

"No," Anna murmured. Joe shook his head. "We wouldn't want that."

This is moving along way too fast. Gracie thought. "How about something to eat?" she asked, standing. "After all that talking and pacing, you must be hungry, Mr. Houston."

"Call me Arnie. But really, all I want's to get cracking on this Lazy Lake deal." He snapped his fingers. "One signature and I'm outta here."

She smiled. "Oh, I think the networks can wait a little longer, don't you, Joe?"

"Well," Joe replied doubtfully.

"Do you think so?" Anna asked.

"Of course, they can," Uncle Miltie added. "Everyone has time for a coffee break."

"This is all very new and exciting. Wonderful news, in fact," Gracie said. "But don't you think you should get some advice, Anna? Joe? Speak to a few people like Rocky Gravino and Ann O'Neill or even my niece Carter. I'm sure, Arnie, as a businessman, you'd recommend a sensible approach to your prospective clients?"

Houston stopped pacing and started blinking. "Uh, well . . ."

"Don't know about the rest of you but I'm ready for something a little less high-pressure. Like a cup of coffee." Uncle Miltie was asserting his own agenda. Gracie bit back a smile. Her uncle stood and grabbed his walker. "Come on, Anna. I hear some banana-fig cupcakes singing our song."

GRACIE WASN'T SURE if it was the offer of cupcakes or her plain-jane coffee or the return of Gooseberry for a late afternoon snack. But soon after they had moved on into the kitchen, Arnie Houston had reluctantly given up trying to get Anna to sign the contract immediately. After much discussion and several cell phone call interruptions, the young agent had finally agreed to give her forty-eight hours to seek some advice. Gracie called Cordelia Fountain and booked him a room. As he left, Arnie Houston warned the Searfosses again that he really couldn't wait much longer. Every minute counted when it came to offering new product, and, although a series based on Anna's books was a fantastic concept, there was always another, equally fantastic, in the offing.

Now, an hour later, Anna had succumbed to Joe and Gracie's combined pressure and gone to rest. Gracie had called Ann McNeill, a lawyer and town councillor. This professional woman immediately expressed her concern for the Searfosses. "They must have been terrified," she said, referring to the fire.

Gracie agreed it had been a horrible experience for them all.

"You went in after them, Gracie?" Ann asked. "And pulled them out of a burning building? Wow, I can't imagine how much courage that must have taken."

Embarrassed by the praise, Gracie said something noncommittal.

"Oh, by the way, I spoke with Mayor Ritter. I just love your suggestion about honoring Anna! I've volunteered to be on the planning committee with you. After he ran the idea by me, I phoned my mom. She read all of Anna's books when she was little. Loved them! I was too interested in superhero comics to give them a chance, can you believe that?" Gracie laughed. "I think my mom may even have them stored somewhere in the attic. Wouldn't that be something? She could bring them to the ceremony. Maybe Anna would sign them?"

"I'm sure she'd be thrilled, Ann," Gracie replied. "That's part of the reason for my call. Anna and Joe have just been approached by an agent. He wants to represent her work, says he can get a television show made."

The lawyer's voice became serious. "He's offered them a contract?"

"Yes, and is pushing hard for them to sign. We . . . er . . . they were hoping you'd look it over. Give them some advice."

"I'd be delighted. Contracts for intellectual property can be tricky."

Ann McNeill agreed to drop around to visit the Searfosses and review the contract first thing Monday morning.

Then Gracie remembered Katie and left a message on the Nickolsons' answering machine regarding the minor incident with Houston. After helping cut onions and carrots and peeling Yukon gold potatoes for her favorite shepherd's pie recipe, Uncle Miltie and Joe had retired to the living room to watch the early news.

Gracie stood at her kitchen counter, keeping an eye on the boiling pots and sizzling lean ground beef, while dicing boiled eggs for a spinach salad. She loved being in her kitchen. The sound of a sharp knife squeaking across green beans, the smell of a curly lemon peel, the sight of a perfectly rising soufflé, all brought great joy and comfort to Gracie's life. Her hands busy, her mind free to roam, she had solved many problems while whipping up a tasty and wholesome meal. Today, though, as she considered the recent events in the Searfosses' lives, she came up with nothing but a healthy suspicion.

First, there was the out-of-the-blue arrival of Tom Williams and his familial claim. Then the sudden appearance of Arnie Houston, who seemed just a *little* too eager to have Anna and

Joe sign. *That boy could talk the talk,* she thought, *but would he walk the walk?* And finally, why was someone deliberately setting the fires in Willow Bend? As she crushed the potatoes, she realized that these uneasy feelings were more intuition than fact.

In no time, she had added dry milk for extra calcium, layered the steaming ingredients into a large loaf pan and pushed it into the oven, along with a tangy blueberry cobbler. With the spinach salad waiting in the fridge, Gracie was making last-minute touch-ups to the dining room settings when the front door bell rang. Their guest was early.

She heard Uncle Miltie open the door as she wiped her hands and removed her apron. "Welcome, Mr. Williams," she said, walking down the hall.

"Please, Mrs. Parks," the Searfosses' nephew replied. "Call me Tom."

After greeting Joe, they settled in the living room. As the visitor earnestly began to tell Joe and Uncle Miltie how much he enjoyed Willow Bend, Gracie gave him the once-over and was pleased that, despite the heat, he was neatly dressed in black slacks and a white shirt and tie. Tom jumped up when Anna entered the room. With a couple of long strides, he was beside her, gently guiding her to a nearby chair.

"Tommy! How lovely that you've come," she said, receiving his gentle kiss on the cheek. "Joe and I were so looking forward to talking to you, weren't we, Joe?"

"Of course," her husband replied. "We've got years of catching up."

While they chatted about Willow Bend, Gracie excused herself. Offering to get drinks, Uncle Miltie joined her.

"Some day!" he said, slowly pulling glasses from the cupboard. "Not sure what to make of all this." He poured iced tea. "Joe says they're both in shock. Too much is happening to them, Gracie. I don't think they know which way is up."

"It's been an awful lot of excitement, that's for sure," she replied, checking the main dish. The potato topping was nicely crisp. She removed the bubbling blueberry cobbler and set it aside. "I'm worried about Anna's health. This kind of stress could really hurt her."

Placing glasses on a tray, her uncle asked, "You still doubt Tom's story?"

Gracie paused for a moment then scowled. "I know you'll laugh and call me on my sleuthing addiction, but . . . something's not right about that man. But I still can't put my finger on just what it is. Yet." She picked up the tray and they returned to the living room.

"Dinner'll be ready in about fifteen minutes," she said, handing round the iced tea.

Tom finished his in one gulp. "That's great. I'm famished. My aunt tells me that not only are you an excellent cook, you're a fine singer."

Gracie smiled. "Oh, I don't know about that, but I do enjoy singing God's praises with our church choir."

"Eternal Hope, right? I understand that my aunt and uncle were founding members." Anna nodded, obviously pleased. "As my aunt reminded me, I used to sing as a boy." He hesitated. "I . . . I admit it's been a while since I've been to church, but I'd love to hear your group."

"That's easy," she replied. "We're singing at tomorrow's service. Would you like to accompany your aunt and uncle?"

"Great. Hey, maybe I can join? Get to know some of the community."

"Well," Gracie said, taken aback. "Ah, perhaps, come tomorrow and I'll ask, okay?"

"We were just going to tell Tom our news," Anna said. "Weren't we, Joe?"

"News?"

Joe nodded. "Anna's been approached by an agent. He thinks he can sell the Lazy Lake books as a children's television show."

There was a thud, followed by the sound of breaking glass. "Oh, I'm sorry!" Tom said, his face white. "It . . . it just slipped. I'm so sorry, Mrs. Parks."

Gracie was up. "It's all right. Just a glass. Now, nobody move for a moment." She quickly brought the broom and swept up the shards while Tom continued to apologize. "There," she said. "Now, anybody hungry?"

"Starved," Uncle Miltie replied.

"Me, too," Joe said, helping Anna into the dining room.

The conversation centered around the food for a while. The casserole was a big hit—they all agreed it was a classic—but talk soon returned to the Searfosses' news. As Gracie offered a second helping, Tom refused, then asked about the agent.

"Could talk the hind leg off a donkey," Uncle Miltie said. "Half the time, he carried on two conversations, one with us, the other on that fancy cell phone that looked like it came from Fort Knox."

"He said he was plugged in to all the family-oriented networks," Joe added, nodding vigorously. "Had contacts everywhere. He said they needed what he called 'product'." He patted his wife's hand. "And my Anna's books were made to order. Offered her a contract on the spot! Didn't he?"

"Sure did," agreed Uncle Miltie, with a polite little burp.

Tom's hand stopped in mid-air, a mushroom dangled precariously from his fork. "Uh . . . did you sign it?"

Joe shook his head.

"Gracie very wisely suggested that we have a lawyer review it first," Anna said, wiping her mouth.

Tom rapidly downed his third glass of ice water. "I think I will have some more of that fabulous shepherd's pie, if I may, Mrs. Parks?" He watched Gracie spoon out a generous portion. "How much time did he give you to consider?"

"Forty-eight hours," Anna replied. "We're seeing the lawyer bright and early Monday morning."

"That little Arnie . . . he wanted twenty-four." Joe shook his head.

"Uh . . . little *Arnie*?" Tom asked, his voice a bit strangled. He cleared his throat.

Joe nodded. "Houston. Arnie Houston he called himself. From the Houston Entertainment Agency." He snorted. "Fancy name for a kid still wet behind the ears. Seemed to know what he was about, though."

Gracie noticed Tom swallow hard, then he pushed his plate aside. "I'm sorry, Mrs. Parks. Guess I wasn't as hungry as I thought."

"That's all right," Gracie replied evenly. "Give you more room for dessert. And please, Tom, call me Gracie."

"Imagine forgetting the Lord's Day," Joe said. "What's this world coming to?"

"Don't rightly know," Uncle Miltie replied. "But sometimes I feel it's passing me by." The others murmured assent. Gracie began clearing the table and asked for a show of hands for coffee. For a moment, Tom seemed lost in thought. Then he jumped up and carried the used dishes to the kitchen.

Uncle Miltie winked. "But not before I get a taste of my niece's blueberry cobbler!"

16

THE RIVER OF GOD sets our feet a dancing. The river of God fills our hearts with cheer. The river of God fills our mouths with laughter. And we rejoice, for the river is here."

Gracie loved this old hymn, especially as a closing song. Though short in length, its rhythm and message were strong. Her choir used both to their advantage. Like jubilant campers around a roaring fire, the Eternal Hope Community Church choir sang "The River Is Here" in many parts, each category of voices separately singing the refrain, then being joined by the others. First, the sopranos sang alone, rising to dizzying heights, followed quickly by the richness of the altos and tenors, softening and coloring the overall sound. Finally, both were boosted by the powerful resonance of the basses and baritones. Then, seventeen-year-old Amy Cantrell's soaring soprano started them all over again. Gracie inhaled, waiting for her mark. Lester Twomley tossed her a wink as the tenors anticipated their second refrain. She returned the gesture then opened her mouth to join the blonde teenager and the others in another rousing chorus.

Soon, the entire congregation swayed to the rocking music, some waving their church bulletins as fans against the unseasonal heat. Then the choir, sitting in the loft above, began clapping in time as they repeated the song. The multiple bangles lining Marge Lawrence's wrists clinked daintily. From the altar below, Pastor Paul Meyer smiled and joined in. The sanctuary reverberated with the sounds of pounding palms and thunderous tongues, punctuated by an occasional "Hallelujah!" Gracie noticed that Tom Williams, sitting with his aunt and uncle, was singing with all his might. As she waited for the tenors and altos to finish, she caught a bit of his voice, a vivid baritone.

Finally, Barb Jennings pounded the last few notes on the old organ. For a moment, the voices stopped, and the air in the church hummed with the final few bars. Pastor Paul thanked everyone for coming and reminded them about the coming week's prayer needs. "Don't forget to thank and praise God," he added, raising his arms in dismissal. "A special welcome to Tom Williams, nephew of Anna and Joe Searfoss." Paul looked down and smiled at the Searfosses. Then he raised his hands. "Very special prayers of thanks to

Lester Twomley and Don Delano and the rest of our wonderful choir for saving our precious church from the recent fire. I don't know what we'd have done without them. I only know I praise and thank the Lord for their calm minds and quick action."

The congregation clapped heartily. The members of the choir smiled and bowed in unison.

"And more thanks—we've been very graced this week, haven't we?—to our Savior for the dear lives of two of our founding members, Anna and Joe Searfoss."

From their seats near the front, Anna smiled while Joe blushed. The clapping grew louder. Sitting beside Anna, Tom Williams bowed his head.

"I understand we have another hero in our midst. Our very own Gracie Parks who helped pull Anna and Joe to safety. Thank God for you all."

Joe stood and looked up at the loft toward Gracie. Marge and Tish pushed a reluctant Gracie to the front where she smiled and scurried back. She hadn't expected this accolade, though she appreciated her pastor's thoughtfulness. The church echoed with the sounds of people standing and shouting, "Hallelujah!" and "Way to go, Gracie!"

"Finally, remember: love one another," the minister continued, arms still high. "Make your lives in the river of God real, living and vital, okay?"

There was a resounding reply of amens followed by the

slamming of hymnbooks and squeaking of shoes as the members slowly trickled out the main doors into the sticky air. Though Pastor Paul was young, and had expressed to her some self-doubt regarding his pastoral capabilities, Gracie always found that he left the congregation with a strong, positive message. Given time, she believed, his confidence would grow and he would tackle some of the more challenging theological and social issues of the day. In the interim, there was nothing wrong with nurturing his flock with simple expressions of love and hope. After all, someone just as young had preached exactly the same messages two thousand years ago.

"Well done, everyone," Barb Jennings said, rising and stretching at the organ. "The 'River' finale was wonderful. Nobody missed their mark."

"A miracle," quipped Don Delano, pulling his robe over his head. Lester Twomley and Rick Harding grinned and followed suit. Rick assisted Lester as his hands were still bandaged. "Glad to have that off," Don added. "Any longer and I'd have melted."

"So that's Anna and Joe's nephew," Estelle said.

"He's kind of cute," Marge added. "Though a little on the skinny side."

Gracie tucked her music sheets into a bag. "Hang on, everybody," she said. "Before you go, I've got a couple of things. The Searfosses' house suffered considerable damage."

Everyone nodded, their faces suddenly serious. Tish Ball

and Tyne Anderson simultaneously whispered, "So sad."

"Well, I wondered if we might consider making a benefit CD, with the proceeds going to Anna and Joe." She paused. "They have insurance—"

"Praise God," Estelle said.

"Amen. But we all know there'll be hidden costs. I thought, if we could swing it, the CD might make a little extra for them and be a good experience for us. What do you think?"

The choir members were silent for a moment. Gracie wondered if she'd made a mistake.

"That's a great idea, Gracie," Don said, finally.

She smiled and gave him a hug.

"Sounds like a lot of fun," Lester added, opening his arms. Gracie chuckled and embraced him as well. The others nodded enthusiastically as they packed up their belongings.

"Will there be solo opportunities?" Estelle asked.

Lester groaned, then fiddled with his bandages to cover the predictable exasperation he felt at Estelle's diva-dom.

"I really haven't thought that far ahead," Gracie replied. "Just wanted to run the idea by you first, check your reaction."

"Think we're all keen," Barb said. A bunch of heads bobbed. "We can choose a selection of old and new favorites. That'd be fun."

"Thank you, my friends, for your generous spirit. Anna

and Joe will be so touched," Gracie replied, her heart swelling. Doing the Lord's work wasn't difficult when you had the support of good people. "I knew I could count on you to help out. I'll try and find out what it entails and get back to you, okay?"

"I'll give you a hand," Lester said. His eyes followed theirs to his own bandaged fingers. "Well, not these ones exactly . . ."

The twins chuckled. Tish prodded him in the stomach.

"Count me in," Don added, pulling on his sunglasses. "I've always wanted to be a record producer."

Everyone laughed and then trooped toward the exit stairway. "Oh! One other thing," Gracie said, spinning around. "Just a quick reminder of the veterans' memorial display unveiling at the seniors center, this Tuesday evening at seven. Marge and I are making treats. Both you and your families are all welcome. If you could just let one of us know if you're coming, we'll have a better idea how much to bring."

"Comfort and I'll be there," Rick said. "We may even splurge and hire a baby-sitter."

"Woo, woo," Don replied. "Big night out for the Hardings."

Rick grinned.

"I'll baby-sit, if you like," Amy offered. She looked at Gracie and shrugged apologetically. "I'd help out, Gracie, but I could really use the cash."

Gracie smiled as Rick and Amy agreed on arrangements.

She heard footsteps coming up into the loft, felt a hand on her shoulder and turned.

"Hi, Mrs. Parks," Tom Williams said, his foot tapping the top step. "Gracie, I mean. Just wanted to tell you and the others how much I enjoyed your performance."

"Thank you," a couple of choir members murmured. Marge Lawrence patted her hair and turned on a brilliant smile. Her bangles tinkled again.

"May I introduce Tom Williams," Gracie said. "As you've heard, he's Anna and Joe's nephew."

Tom shook the men's hands and bowed slightly to the women as they introduced themeselves. "So pleased to meet you all. My aunt and uncle are very lucky to have such good friends." His narrow face darkened for a moment. "Willow Bend's a really nice town."

Marge took his arm. "Where are you from? I was fascinated to hear that Anna and Joe had a nephew."

He nodded. "We'd lost touch, but we're back together again. And what do you do, Mrs. Lawrence?"

"Oh, call me Marge." She fluttered her big eyes. "I own a little gift shop in town. You should drop by sometime."

He smiled. "Thank you. I might just do that."

"Are you going to be—" Tish started.

"Here for long?" Tyne finished.

Tom smiled at the twins. "I'm not sure, but I'd love to join the choir while I'm around. Do you think that's possible?"

Everyone looked at Barb. The choir director flushed. "Well, it's a bit unusual but . . . I guess we could use another voice."

"Course we could," Marge piped in. "Our choir's open to anyone who wants to sing God's praises, right?"

Marybeth and the twins nodded.

"Baritone, is it?" Barb asked.

Tom nodded.

Don clapped him on the back. "Great to have you on board, Tom. Sometimes I'm all alone, bringing depth to this bunch of voices."

"Hey!" Lester squeaked.

"See what I mean?"

They all roared with laughter. Even Lester.

TOM OFFERED TO DROP Uncle Miltie at a friend's house for a chat, then take his aunt and uncle for lunch and a drive around the countryside. Delighted to have a bit of time to herself, Gracie carefully hung up her choir robe with the others, bid her good-byes and stepped outside to embrace the heat wave. Herb Bower met her at the bottom of the church steps.

"Hi, Gracie," the police chief said. "Hope you don't mind my waiting, but we haven't had a chance to talk about the fire at the Searfosses. I know it's Sunday and all, but have you a moment?"

The last thing Gracie wanted to do was relive those terrible minutes, but she nodded and sat down on a step.

The big man pulled out a small notepad and joined her. "Now, if you'd just tell me what happened, from the beginning. How'd you happen to be there, in the first place?"

Gracie swallowed the thick, warm air while arranging her thoughts. "It was just a coincidence. I know. I know," she said quickly, as an expression of doubt crossed his handsome face. "We've had one too many of those. But, if it *wasn't* plain old coincidence," she turned and glanced at the church's entrance, "it was divine intervention. Gooseberry and I were walking, just to get some air, when I turned the corner and found I was staring at the Searfosses' front door."

"What'd you see?"

"Nothing out of the ordinary, at first. I *smelled* smoke, then just as I was beginning to realize it was coming from Anna and Joe's . . ."

"Yes?"

Gracie shrugged. "Tom Williams burst out the front door and nearly knocked me over running away! For a minute, I was stunned. Then I just raced up the stairs, shouting for Anna and Joe." She paused, momentarily overcome by the memories. It was as though the smoke filled her nostrils once again.

Herb squeezed her shoulder. "Then what?"

"I fell to my knees, the smoke was everywhere. Couldn't see. I kept yelling 'Joe! Anna!' and then I heard Joe's voice directing me to the living room. Thank the Lord!" She swallowed hard. "It was really hot, difficult to breathe, but somehow we bumped into each other and Joe and I helped Anna out." She paused, disoriented by the bright sunlight.

"And then what?"

"It was very confusing. The fire truck was there, men shouting, rushing around with hoses, Rick was offering help. A while later, I saw you." She shrugged. "You know the rest."

"Let me get this straight," he said, jotting something in his booklet. "You're certain that Tom Williams came *out* the front door?"

She nodded. "Went right past me."

"Could he have been going in and then turned round?"

Gracie considered the question. "Can't say for certain but I don't think so. Why? Is it important?" He told me he panicked.

"Don't rightly know, at the moment," Herb replied. He wiped his brow and shoved the notebook into his pocket. "Well, thanks, Gracie. Sorry to keep you." He stood. "If you remember anything else, you'll let me know, right?"

She nodded and accepted his offered hand, then rose. He walked her to her car and waved good-bye as she climbed into Fannie Mae. For a while, she just sat, trying to think. After a few minutes, all she had discovered was heat and hunger. She turned the key and steered her old Cadillac into a parking spot in front of Abe's Deli. Abe Wasserman's superb home cooking was almost as well known as the cheerful owner's always heartening conversation. Now Gracie had a hankering for both. She laughed when she saw Rocky Gravino's tiny black sedan parked a couple of spots over. His two dogs, Rover and Gent—their heads thrust through the sunroof—whimpered excitedly as she tickled their noses.

"Hi ya, Gracie! Hot enough for you?" Abe asked, pleased, as always, to see her. He moved from around the counter to give her a brief hug. "Counter or table?"

As usual, several tables were already taken as well as half the counter stools. Gracie waved at several familiar faces and smiled when she saw Rocky sitting alone near the end of the counter. He stood and called her over. Rocky gave her a quick squeeze around the shoulders. "So glad you're safe," he whispered.

"Thank you, dear Rocky," she replied, taking up residence beside him.

The stocky widower was finishing a double order of Abe's famous blintzes with applesauce. "Really hoped you'd drop by, Gracie." He examined her closely, noticed the bandage on her arm. "Are you sure you're okay?"

She nodded.

"What'll it be for our local hero?" Abe asked, returning to his side of the counter.

Gracie didn't need the menu. "One of your roast turkey sandwiches on whole—"

"Come on, Gracie. After what you've just been through. Time to live a little. Give the little lady *pumpernickel*, Abe," Rocky waged.

Abe looked at her. "Sounds good," Gracie admitted. "Glass

of ice water and a small order of coleslaw, if you don't mind."

"Mind? It's what I live for," Abe replied with a grin. "Be up in a jiffy."

As Abe prepared her sandwich, Gracie and Rocky chatted about the welfare of their respective animals and then moved on to the subject of the latest news in Willow Bend, including the fires that had culminated in the one at Joe and Anna's.

"Gracie, you never disappoint me," Abe said, joining in. "Pickle?" She nodded. "Pulled them right through the flames."

"Not exactly," she replied, accepting the plate bulging with food. "Mostly just smoke, but I don't mind telling you, I was scared to death. Poor things, they could have died."

"So could've you, Gracie," Rocky said. "As I said before, you shouldn't be taking that kind of risk."

Abe nodded gravely then moved to the cash register to assist a customer.

"I couldn't just stand there, Rocky. You two would've done the same," she replied, turning her attention to lunch. "*Hmm*! Cranberry-mayonnaise. Excellent!" she told Abe upon his return. "I especially like the hint of lemon in the mayo." He smiled, grabbed the coffee pot, filled three mugs and slid one in front of her. She took a sip while he cleared a table and provided another couple with change.

"Have you done any stories about the other fires?" Gracie asked Rocky.

"Others? Oh, you mean the burning trash cans?"

She nodded, sampling the coleslaw. Very tart, as usual, just the way she liked it. She ate heartily.

Rocky shrugged his large shoulders. "One of my guys was looking into it, sort of a page-four news brief. Why?" He leaned closer. "Anything my readers should know?"

Gracie hesitated. She wouldn't lie, but did she really know the truth? Taking a sip of water to gain some time, she decided to keep quiet. No sense in stirring the pot. She shook her head and scooped up the last shreds of slaw.

Now, the deli was almost empty. Abe settled into the stool beside Gracie and sipped his coffee. "Anna and Joe have had some interesting times, haven't they? Real highs and lows."

She nodded, still chewing her sandwich.

Rocky shifted on his stool. "They're staying with you, right?" Her mouth still full, Gracie nodded again. "Heard they've got some long-lost relative, just arrived out of the blue. Not to mention her books being discovered again. Care to comment?"

Gracie wiped her mouth and swallowed. "To you, Rocky, but not to the *Gazette*, okay?" The salt-and-pepper-haired editor mimed returning a pen to his pocket and placed two fingers over his heart. "Okay," she said. "It's true. Their nephew, Tom Williams, arrived a couple of days ago."

"Nephew?" Abe looked surprised. "The one they lost touch with?"

"That's right, her sister's son." Gracie quickly filled him in on Tom's history and arrival in Willow Bend.

Rocky pursed his lips. "A lot of excitement in that household in a short time." His eyes twinkled. "Or, are you going to tell me that I'm just sniffing for a story." Gracie grinned briefly as Rocky continued. "Can't deny that it would make headlines, though. Sell a few papers."

"No, there's a story here," Gracie admitted. "Frankly, I'm just not sure what to say. Tom seems all right, but I just can't shake the feeling that something's amiss. Uncle Miltie says it's all in my imagination . . ."

It was Abe's turn to smile. "Don't know about that. I've always believed in intuition. Had to. Take my sister, Sophie. Why she's downright amazing sometimes. Just gets these 'premonitions' she calls 'em and, by gum, a lot of the time, she's right."

"Do you know anything about television production?" Gracie asked Rocky as Abe fetched the coffee pot.

Rocky frowned. "Not sure what you mean?"

Gracie fiddled with her mug. "Not very sure myself, to be honest, but I was just wondering how hard it was to get a show produced."

"Well," Rocky started, leaning back slightly, "used to know a guy who worked in New York for one of the big three. Now it's more like the big three hundred."

Gracie blinked.

"Networks. Now cable. Whatever it is, it's still all a matter of contacts and timing. Of course, you have to have the right vehicle, but those who know how and to whom to pitch, and when, seem to be the key. You can make a pile of money, though. Especially if your show goes into syndication. Why?" He looked at her with amusement. "You going to be on TV?"

"Who's going to be on TV?" Abe asked, offering them a refill.

They both shook their heads. "I'm so full," Gracie said. "I could—hey! Do you smell smoke?"

Abe sniffed then cocked his head. "Out the back!" he cried, on the run.

When Gracie and Rocky caught up with him in the alley, Abe was already beating a flaming trash can with his apron. "Fire extinguisher! Inside the back door," he shouted.

Rocky whirled, raced back inside and returned seconds later with a bright red tube. Abe grabbed it, and sprayed immediately. The thick shower of white foam drowned the blaze. The trio stood, breathing heavily, and waited until they were certain the flames were extinguished.

"What a funny thing," Abe said, glancing up and down the empty alley. "Never happened before." He peered into the blackened sludge filling the can. "Can't imagine what caused it."

"I can," Gracie replied. Rocky's mouth opened in surprise. "Come on, Abe. You've got to call Herb Bower."

THIS'LL BE THE FIFTH INCIDENT in the past month,"
Herb Bower said, gratefully accepting a cup of coffee.
The four of them sat in a booth near the door.

"Fifth?" Rocky asked. "Know about Barry's, Gracie's church, and now Abe's trash can. What're the others?"

The chief of police glanced around the deli. They were alone except for a young couple paying more attention to each other than to their respective milkshakes, much less the knot of old-timers chin-wagging near the entrance. "Well, the first was a fire at Anderson's, and then, of course, we're not sure here, but you've also got the Searfosses'."

"The meat market had a fire?" Gracie asked. "I didn't realize."

Herb shrugged. "At the time, it was no big deal but now—"

He took another gulp of coffee. "Good coffee, Abe." He bit into a honey-almond cookie.

The deli owner nodded in acknowledgment and again offered the steaming black liquid to the others, but they declined.

"As I was saying, at first, no big deal." Herb lowered his voice. "Now, things have taken a different tack. Looks like we may have a serial arsonist on our hands."

"A what?" Gracie exclaimed.

"Some nut who gets his jollies from playing with matches," Rocky said.

"You think someone's deliberating setting these fires?" Abe asked. "In Willow Bend?"

"You did think the church fire was deliberately set," Gracie said, her voice slightly accusatory.

Herb shrugged his massive shoulders. "Sorry, didn't want to say anything at the time. But, yeah, sure looks like it now," Herb said. "Too coincidental to be accidents. Modus operandi's the same: small, easily set, contained fires in quiet locations."

"You're forgetting the Searfosses," Gracie said. "That wasn't small nor contained."

The cookie in Herb's right hand went up and down. "Why I said we're not sure about that one. Why we're keeping it quiet. Sometimes these characters need to escalate. You know, each time the thrill's harder to get so they have to make it more exciting, more dangerous. The bigger the splash, the sooner they'll jump back into the water. Could be what happened at the Searfosses'."

"But to risk killing people?" Gracie asked. "I know I'm ignorant of the motivations behind arson, but it would seem there's a world of difference between setting trash cans on fire and torching an occupied home."

"He may not have known it was occupied," Rocky said. "Maybe it was just bad luck."

They both looked at Herb. The chief shrugged again. "We really don't know, but until we get the answer, we're treating it, along with all the others, as suspicious."

"Who would do such a terrible thing?" Gracie asked.

"Sadly, they're all kinds of folks. These fires don't seem to have any insurance or fraud motivations—" He hesitated. "Unless you've got something to tell me, Abe?" Abe put up his hands in mock defeat. "Didn't think so. No, this kind of fire-setting's usually done by kids. Bored, looking for thrills and attention. You didn't see anybody in the alley?"

"No," Abe replied. "Deserted by the time we got there." Gracie and Rocky shook their heads.

"Too bad. Sometimes the arsonist hangs around. They like watching the results of their work, so they're often in the crowd. It's amazing, really. A fire marshal in Chicago told me that if you can catch them and pump them on the spot, sometimes they'll up and admit it." He stirred his coffee for a moment. "Know it sounds weird, but they're so desperate for attention, they'll settle for the negative kind."

Gracie shook her head. "Poor things," she said. "You mean all they really need is some old-fashioned love."

Rocky raised his eyebrows. "Ever the optimist, my dear. I can think of half a dozen things I think they need. Not one of them is love, I assure you."

She patted his hand. "Don't forget, Rocky. We may not be able to direct the wind, but we can adjust the sail. This child needs to know he's loved." Abe murmured his agreement.

"You said 'he.' Interesting," Rocky said. "Are arsonists usually male?"

"That's my understanding," Herb said. "I take Gracie's point, though. Sometimes the kid's having trouble at school or home, you know the kind of thing. Resolve that and usually the fire-setting stops." He frowned.

"What?" Abe asked.

"Course, there's always the possibility that, if not dealt with quickly, it'll become a habit. An obsession, even." He exhaled heavily. "Could go on into adulthood, each incident getting larger, more deadly."

"Don't like the sound of that," Abe said.

"Dear me, no," Gracie added.

THAT PORK ROAST SMELLS LOVELY," Anna Searfoss said.

Gracie laughed and continued sautéing apples. "What's really lovely is the sandwiches we can have tomorrow."

"I think it's about time to check it," Anna said, shifting in her kitchen chair. "It's been almost an hour."

"Already? My word, Anna! Time goes by when you're enjoying good company." Gracie wiped her hands on her apron, tugged on thick mitts and opened the oven door.

Her friend smiled. "Oh! I can smell the rosemary and garlic even more now!"

"Too much?" Gracie asked.

"No." Anna sniffed delicately. "Too mouth-watering is all."

Gracie pulled the pan out of the oven, and drained off the

excess fat. She joined Anna at the table. "Has to stand for a few minutes."

Anna reached across for her friend's arm. "I can't thank you enough for being so good to Joe and me. And to Tommy! He said you're going to let him sing in the choir." She clapped her hands together. "How wonderful to have him a member of our church."

Gracie agreed. "I'm glad you had the day together."

"Yes," Anna said. "We talked about all sorts of things. He's very interested in my work, you know."

"Is he?" Gracie replied, keeping the doubt from her voice. "In what way?"

"Oh, he wanted to know about the New York publisher, wanted to be sure that Joe and I are getting the best deal. He's very keen on the TV idea but . . ." Her voice trailed off.

"Excuse me for a moment." Gracie rose and slid the roast onto the platter awaiting it. She poked her head into the living room where Uncle Miltie and Joe were watching the news. Raising her voice over the din, she gave them the five-minute warning. "But what, dear?" she asked Anna.

"He's not too keen on Arnie Houston," Anna said. "Says we should take our time, maybe even talk to some other agents."

"That sounds like good advice," Gracie said. "After all, you're the one with the 'product,' as they call it. Not the other way around. Why don't you ask Ann tomorrow? She has a friend in entertainment contracts law in Chicago," she said.

Anna's face brightened.

At that moment, Joe and Uncle Miltie marched in. "Smells wonderful!" Joe said, taking his wife's arm. "What is it?"

"Roast pork and apples with rice pilaf and glazed sprouts. Brussels, that is."

Joe's eyes widened appreciatively. Anna smiled broadly. "A little more of Gracie's hospitality and we're never going to want to leave."

Gracie grinned and began slicing the roast.

"What about me?" Uncle Miltie asked, taking Anna's other arm. "We're a package deal, you know. Aren't we, my dear?"

Gracie followed them into the dining room. "Praise God. We certainly are."

As Joe began to serve, Gracie nipped back into the kitchen to turn off the oven and take off her apron.

To her delight, the pork dish was a resounding success. Both Uncle Miltie and Joe had second portions, but she was pleased to see that enough remained for tomorrow's lunch. Uncle Miltie adored sliced pork sandwiches.

As the men cleared the table, Gracie busied herself with making coffee and cutting the dessert. The doorbell rang. As she headed down the hall, she heard a short, intense squeal followed quickly by a high-pitched caterwaul. Startled, she quickly opened the front door. Tom Williams stared at her, his mouth partially open.

"What was that?" he sputtered.

Gooseberry burst through as though fired from a rocket. Crying pitifully, he raced up and down the hallway then shot into the living room and dove under an armchair. The tip of his pumpkin-colored tail peeked out.

"What's going on?" Uncle Miltie shouted.

"Gooseberry!" Gracie cried. "Oh, come in, Tom," she said, turning away. "Excuse me."

"Something wrong with your cat?" Joe asked, as he entered the hallway. "Hello, Tom! What a surprise! How good to see you."

Tom Williams smiled and stepped into the hallway.

Joe stuck out his hand, then hesitated. "Smells a bit like burnt hair or something."

"It's the cat," Tom replied. "Flew in like his tail's on fire."

Gracie barely heard them. She was in the living room, on her knees, trying to reach her beloved feline. "Come on, Goosie. What's wrong?" She stretched to rub his chin but he moved farther away. In the shadow under the chair, his green eyes were huge and staring. "Come on, Sweetie." Gracie stroked his tummy, feeling for a heartbeat. There was an accelerated thump, thump, thump against her palm. For a couple of minutes, she whispered softly to him and was delighted when rewarded finally by a soft meow. She then grabbed the fur around his neck and gently pulled him into the open. She accidentally brushed his tail and he shrieked again. "Oh, my handsome Goosie," she said, examining the long plume of orange fluff. "What's happened to your beautiful tail?"

There was an ugly, dark splotch of burnt fur where the fluffy tip used to be. Gracie peered carefully. No blood. Gently, she examined the rest of him, then exhaled heavily. "I think he's okay," she said as the others crowded around. She stood and rubbed her cat's chin. He purred lightly. *Thank You, Lord*, she whispered.

"What in tarnation do you think happened?" Uncle Miltie asked.

"I've no idea," she replied. "He's been burned—oh, dear!" She gently placed Gooseberry on the chair. "The arsonist! Quick, we've got to check outside."

"The what?" both Joe and Uncle Miltie cried. But she was already halfway down the hall, charging past a startled Tom Williams.

Once outside, Gracie inhaled the the humid night air, thick with the scents of late spring and . . . something else. Smoke! Swallowing her rising dread, she sniffed and looked quickly around. It took her a couple of seconds to adjust to the darkness. The moon had yet to rise, but there were pools of light spilling around the street lamps. She narrowed her eyes and followed her nose. Crossing her driveway, she noticed a charcoal haze rising from the side of her garage! Joe and Tom suddenly arrived as she rounded the wall. Short yellow flames shot up from a small clump of rags, nestled danger-ously close to the wall of her wooden garage. Joe and Tom began stamping on the flames, then Gracie joined in.

"I've got the hose," Uncle Miltie shouted from a distance.

Gracie darted back to him, grabbed it from him and untwisted it, saturating herself. Fighting panic, she aimed the spewing water onto the rags and quickly doused the flames. Joe raked the sodden mess away from the wall, while Tom used the hose to drench it again. They offered to stand guard for a few minutes to make sure the flames were completely extinguished. Uncle Miltie handed Tom a shovel which he used to push the smouldering ash back and forth, looking for hot spots.

"Why would anyone do this?" Gracie asked, her voice filled with pain.

Joe shook his head. Her uncle squeezed her shoulder. "Some prank," he replied. "Just some stupid kid's prank."

She turned to Tom. "Did you see anything? You arrived just as it started."

Tom looked startled. "No, nothing. I just came to the door, the cat flew across the lawn—"

"Hey, you're all wet!" Uncle Miltie interrupted. "You go inside, Gracie," he ordered. "Get changed. We'll handle it out here, okay?"

She nodded, her blouse and curls sopping, and returned to find Anna trembling on her porch.

The elderly woman was almost in hysterics. "What's going on? Where's Joe? I smell smoke. Dear God, is the house on fire?"

"It's all right," Gracie replied, enveloping the shaking woman in her arms. "I'm sorry we left you, Anna. We shouldn't have. It's just a bunch of rags that caught fire, that's all. Nothing to worry about." She turned the woman around. "You're perfectly safe."

"Where's Joe? Where's my Joe?"

"Over here, love," Joe's voice shouted. "Go back inside. Tom's here. Everything's okay. We'll be right there."

Gracie directed the blind woman into the kitchen, while chatting to her gently. "No wonder, you're terrified," she said, helping Anna sit. "After what you've been through." She grabbed an old scarf from behind the back door and draped it like a shawl around her friend's hunched shoulders. "It's all right," she crooned, as though speaking to a child. She poured a glass of orange juice and handed it to Anna. "Everything's all right."

As Anna drank, Gracie checked on Gooseberry. He was curled in a ball, sound asleep. "Poor boy!" she whispered, stroking his head. One green eye opened briefly. She relievedly watched him breathe for a couple of seconds.

Satisfied that he'd survived his trauma, she picked up the phone and dialed Herb Bower's number.

While she listened to the ringing, Gracie watched Gooseberry's downy orange tummy steadily rise and fall. *Lord, I know I've been asking You for a lot lately, but we really need Your help to find this troubled child,* she prayed. *If it is a child. Now, You know I'm here on earth to serve You and do Your will. So, if there's anything I can do, please show me. Please. Before someone gets badly hurt.*

FIFTEEN MINUTES LATER, Herb Bower and Arnie Houston arrived simultaneously.

"It's like Grand Central Station," Uncle Miltie muttered as Gracie, now dressed in a thick sweatshirt and pants combination, greeted both men.

Herb removed his hat. "Awfully glad everything's all right." He gave her hand a quick squeeze then joked, "We've got to stop meeting like this, Gracie."

She smiled briefly and introduced Herb to Arnie. Then, she led the pair to the kitchen where the rest quietly sat around the table. Despite having known the police chief for a long time, Herb Bower's size and confident air sometimes intimidated Gracie. This Sunday evening, however, she found them both comforting.

"Everything under control?" Herb asked, staring at the dazed faces.

Tom looked up, blinked, then stood. "I'm Tom Williams," he said, quickly moving around the table. He shook Herb's hand then moved to Arnie before the chief of police could reply. Arnie Houston opened his mouth in surprise. "Tom Williams," he repeated loudly. "Joe and Anna's nephew."

The young agent frowned. "Tom? What're you—"

"*Very* pleased to meet you," Tom added and vigorously shook Houston's hand. "What did you say your name was?"

"Joe, could you...?" Gracie asked, glancing toward Houston.

"Of course," Joe replied. "Have a seat, Arnie. We've just had a bit of excitement."

Gracie threw him a grateful look and steered Herb out the screen door. As they walked to the garage following the yellow glow from Herb's flashlight, she quickly filled in the chief of police.

"Seems like our old friend," Herb said, kicking gently at the wet clump. He cast his flashlight in a slow three-hundred-sixty-degree roll then slid the beam back near Gracie's face. "Cat okay?" He pulled the beam along the ground and walked away from the fire. Near the garage door, he bent quickly, directing the light up and down.

"Think so, thanks for asking. Find something?"

He pushed back his hat and glanced up. "Uh huh. Some kind of tire track." He stood and wiped his hands on his dark pants.

"Maybe Uncle Miltie's walker."

Herb walked back and grunted in agreement. He placed his hand and the light beam along the wall of the garage directly above the flames. "Not too warm. Can't see any scorch marks. Be clearer in the morning but it looks like you found it in time, praise the Lord." He smacked his lips. "Could've been ugly, Gracie. Garage might have gone up in a flash and then..."

She shivered.

He touched her arm. "Nothing more we can do now. Let's get inside. You've had a nasty shock."

Gracie did feel a bit shaken, but seeing the golden light spilling across her porch and hearing the sound of voices floating out from her kitchen strengthened her inner core of security. It was the part of herself that made her a source of strength for others. Now Gooseberry was safe. She, her uncle and guests were safe. Her dear old house was safe. She whispered a quick prayer of thank you and stepped into her kitchen.

"... the choir could even sing the Lazy Lake theme song," Arnie Houston was saying, pacing along one counter. "Sometimes these songs take off, become an overnight hit. I gotta tell you, Mrs. Searfoss, it could be a bullet. A real money-maker. You know, for your church and all that." He jerked to a halt and looked up.

"Everything all right?" Uncle Miltie asked.

"Uh huh," Herb replied, hat in hand. "Not much more we can do tonight."

"What do you think caused it?" Joe asked. "Gracie mentioned an arsonist."

"Yeah," Uncle Miltie added. "What's that all about."

Herb looked at Gracie. Arnie began drumming his fingers along the counter top.

Gracie shrugged apologetically. "It just popped out, Herb. I'm sorry."

"No problem," he replied. "May I take a seat?"

"Of course!" Gracie exclaimed. "I should have—"

Tom Williams jumped up. "Please, take mine. I'll get anoth—ohhh." He suddenly swayed and would have fallen if Herb's large hands hadn't caught him.

"Tommy!" Anna cried. "What's wrong?"

"Whoa there!" Herb said, gently sliding Tom into his chair. "You all right?"

Tom sat for a moment, his face paler than the rising moon now glowing outside the kitchen window. "I . . . I'm fine, thank you." He exhaled slowly. "Little dizzy. Must have gotten up too quickly, that's all."

"Sure you're all right, then?" Herb asked, as Joe brought in another dining-room chair.

Tom nodded. Gracie handed him a glass of water which he quickly swallowed. He whispered thanks.

Herb sat, carefully placed his hat under his seat, then glanced at Arnie. The young man flushed slightly and slipped into his chair.

"You were going to tell us about an arsonist?" Uncle Miltie prodded.

"In Willow Bend?" Anna asked.

Herb sighed and leaned back. "It's kind of a long story."

"How about over coffee and ice cream?" Gracie asked. "We were just about to have some when . . ." Her voice faded.

"That's a great idea, dear," Uncle Miltie said. "Joe and I'll help out."

Soon, everyone was happily spooning up pistachio or chocolate chip and sipping hot coffee. Between bites, Herb Bower told them about the other fires.

"Uh . . . would you excuse me for just a minute?" Gracie asked, pushing her untouched bowl aside.

Several heads nodded, their overloaded spoons hovering in the air.

She moved around Tom and Herb's chairs, grabbed a cat treat from the cupboard, and slipped into the quiet of her living room. On her own favorite chair near the front window posed Gooseberry. With one hind leg bolt upright, his precious feline majesty was intently licking his stomach.

He glanced up at her, meowed lightly, then returned to his task, ignoring the indignity of a scorched tail.

Gracie placed the treat near him. The licking stopped; the pumpkin head popped up. Gooseberry gently sniffed, then began munching.

Gracie smiled and returned to her guests.

Now, everyone was enjoying dessert.

21

HOW MARVELOUS! HOW WONDERFUL! And my song shall ever be. How marvelous! How wonderful! Is my Savior's love for me."

Barb's baton rattled on the organ. "A little more *oomph!* on the *hows*, please. Especially you tenors."

Rick and Lester exchanged a glance while Tish and Tyne mouthed the word *how*. With their matching pale-blue eyes and frilly outfits, the twins today resembled oversized children. Gracie caught Marybeth's eye and stifled a grin. She needed some light entertainment. She'd spent the morning with the Searfosses and Ann McNeill, discussing Houston's proposed contract. Tongue-twisting phrases like *indemnify against all costs, expenses, losses, liabilities, damages and settlements, does not infringe upon any existing common law rights, proprietary rights, civil rights or any other right whatsoever,* and *assigned, pledged or otherwise encumbered,* still cluttered her brain.

After a confusing hour, the trio had been grateful when Ann had made the offer to review the document at her office and get back to the couple with her advice by early the next day. Just as the lawyer was leaving, Marge arrived. Over a pot of herbal tea, Anna and Joe told her the latest news. Marge was particularly taken with Houston's offer to have the choir sing the proposed television show's theme song. Because of this distraction, Gracie had barely had enough time to do a quick bit of grocery shopping before choir practice.

"Again," Barb commanded.

Though the Eternal Hope choir had been rehearsing "I Stand Amazed" for fifteen minutes, the members dutifully tackled the chorus one more time, each emphatically emphasizing the chosen word.

"Better!" Barb said. "Much better. You see the difference in tempo?" She rapped the baton again. *Taaap. Taaap, tap, tap.* "Charles Gabriel wanted it to be strong. *Very* strong." She peered toward the back. "Another baritone really makes a difference. Thank you, Tom."

The others clapped.

Tom Williams grinned and bowed slightly. "Anything I can do for the group, Barb."

"Speaking of doing things for the group," Marge interjected. "I've got great news."

"I really don't think the timing—" Gracie started.

Marge charged on. "Anna's going to let us sing the theme song for the TV show based on all the Lazy Lake stories."

"What?" the twins cried simultaneously.

"Theme song?" Rick asked.

"Television show!" Lester crowed. He and Rick almost exchanged a high five until Lester remembered his damaged fingers. Instead, the two men shouted, "All right!"

"I get a solo!" Estelle sang out. She paused for a moment, then added, for the benefit of the teen soloist beside her, "I'm sure there'll be more than one, Amy."

Barb's baton thumped wildly. The tapping was ignored as the members huddled together, chatting excitedly.

Gracie groaned. Now there would be no way to get the group back on track.

"It could be even better," Marge said. "Maybe there'll even be real parts in the show? I used to act a bit when I was younger."

Everyone stared at her.

She flushed, played with her hair. "All right. So it was public school, but I was the star!"

"Wore a bit of greasepaint once, myself," Don said. "Still help out at the school plays. Hey, Gracie! Who's staring? Do you think there'll be auditions for parts?"

"You think so?" Amy asked. "Wow! I've always wanted to be in a musical."

"I hope the star's someone like Harrison Ford," Barb said.

"Or Brad Pitt. He's dreamy," Amy added.

Gracie held up her hands. "Wait a minute! Wait a *minute*! I think you're all jumping the gun a little here. Anna and Joe haven't even signed the contract."

"They haven't?" Tom asked. "I thought the lawyer was coming this morning."

Gracie nodded. "She's reading it over now."

"Oh," he replied. "Good for them to seek professional help. Hope she mentioned considering other agencies."

"They've *got* to sign," Estelle declared.

"Maybe the show could be shot in Willow Bend?" Marybeth suggested. Barb and the twins nodded.

"I'm not really sure my aunt's in a position to ask for that," Tom offered.

"Why not?" Estelle asked.

Tom blushed. "I . . . I don't really know. I was just . . ."

"It'd be only natural to have it in the author's hometown," Marybeth continued.

"Wonderful! Wouldn't it be fun for all of us?" Marge exclaimed. "We'd have to make a few changes, so that it looked like the turn of the century but that wouldn't be so hard, would it? Think how lovely it'd look, horse-drawn carriages, ladies in their petticoats, or is it hoop dresses?" She paused, lost in the image. "Hey! Maybe they'll use my shop as a set?" She paused, thinking. "Bet you they pay real well!"

"And Abe's Deli, too," Amy added. "That'll be one time I

wouldn't complain about working. Oh . . . this's so exciting!" The teenager clapped her hands together. "Wait'll I tell my friends! Nothing like this's ever happened in Willow Bend."

Gracie shook her head as the conversations and suggestions continued to spin. She knew, within hours, everyone in Willow Bend would know about the possible television series. Her dear friends Joe and Anna, however, already had enough to worry about. They didn't need the added pressure of a star-struck town.

"YOU'RE SURE SHE CAN'T COME to the phone?" Cordelia Fountain asked. "It's awfully important."

Gracie shifted the receiver to her other ear. Gooseberry glanced up from his nearly empty bowl, pink tongue darting across his lips. She was relieved to see him eating so well. Other than a singed tail tip, there were no lasting effects from the excitement of the previous night. "Is it about Tom?"

"Who? Oh, Tom! No," the owner of the local tourist home replied. "No, it's not about him."

"I'm very sorry, Cordelia, but Anna's unavailable. Would you like to leave a message?"

"No. Yes. Oh, I don't know!" Cordelia paused for a moment. Gracie could hear an old scratchy record playing in the background. "Listen, Gracie, you've heard about her Lazy Lake television show?"

"There isn't—"

Cordelia cut her off. "Well, I want Anna to know there's no hard feelings that she and Joe are staying with you. They know they're always welcome here. Tell her that Fountain's would be a perfect place for the cast to stay. Or," she giggled. Gracie opened her mouth, but Cordelia's voice quickly filled her ear again. "Perhaps, even as a set. Doesn't matter. *Whatever* Anna needs. You just tell her Cordelia stands ready to provide. Would you tell her that? And ask her to call me? Soon as possible?"

Gracie glanced at Anna and Joe, sitting quietly across from her at the kitchen table. Anna's plate of lasagna and Caesar salad was untouched. Cordelia's was the fourth phone call for her friend in less than an hour. First, Jessica Larson, president of the Eternal Hope board, had called to "encourage" Anna to demand that the television series be shot in Willow Bend, using their church. Anna had become so upset at Jessica's pushiness that she had put down the phone and started to cry.

Then Gracie began running interference. When Phil Murphy, the high school band director, called, Gracie told him that Anna was unavailable. But the man whose license plate read *TOOTLE* wouldn't let her go until Gracie agreed to ask Anna to consider using the band in the series. Then Lucille Murphy called, ostensibly just to congratulate Anna. But when Anna couldn't come to the phone, Lucille asked Gracie to make sure Anna and Joe didn't sign anything unless they'd been promised the series would be shot in Willow Bend. It made no difference when Gracie replied that location wasn't even an option on the bargaining table. For the police dispatcher, it was an open-and-shut case. What a way to put their little town on the national map! Gracie was fiddling with the answering machine, to turn down the volume so they wouldn't hear the voice of the caller, when Cordelia rang.

"Not again," Uncle Miltie replied, shaking his head.

Anna, her eyes still red, pushed aside her plate.

"You've got to eat, darling," Joe said, sliding the plate back in front of her. "Please. Just a mouthful."

"Come on, old girl," Uncle Miltie added, swallowing. "The salad is really delicious. Especially with the homemade croutons."

"I'll tell her. Yes. Good-bye," Gracie sighed, hung up the phone, then collapsed in her chair. Gooseberry trotted into the living room. "Oh, Anna! I'm so sorry. Everyone seems to have gone crazy."

The phone rang again. Joe and Uncle Miltie groaned. Anna's bottom lip quivered.

Gracie jumped up and flipped off the ringer. The quartet sat, waiting. The answering machine clicked, then silently began taking a message.

"Pass me the salad, Joe?" Gracie asked, changing the subject. "And tell Anna how dashing Uncle Miltie looks in his old uniform jacket."

For a moment, no one moved. Then Joe grinned and handed over the large bowl. "Like a million bucks!"

"Ha!" Uncle Miltie exclaimed. "I would if I could only get the darn thing on." He glanced ruefully at his sagging stomach. "Not exactly in fighting trim."

A hint of a smile raced across Anna's face. The other three exchanged grateful looks.

"How about you get your jacket out after dinner and we'll have a look?" Gracie suggested. "I can probably open a seam or two," she added delicately. Joe grinned. "I'm sure you'll be very impressive. Don't you think, Anna?"

The elderly woman's smile widened. She slowly started cutting into her lasagna. "Yes. There's something about a man in a uniform."

"I remember one fellow. From Georgia, I think," Uncle Miltie said. "Skinny as a flagpole—uniform practically hung on him—but could he eat! My word, that boy would swallow the beans cold. Right out of the tin. And this was in the kitchen. He was the cook, if you can believe it!" He chuckled. "Still think of him everytime Gracie opens a can of baked beans."

To the others' relief and delight, Anna slowly ate, stopping only when she had to laugh.

The conversation remained light, with Joe and Uncle Miltie trying to one-up each other with more reminiscences about mess-hall meals and rations during the war.

With half of her meal remaining, Anna stopped. "Would you mind, Gracie, if I went to our room for a while? I'm feeling a little tired."

"Of course," Gracie replied. "You sure you're all right?"

Anna nodded then Joe helped her from the table.

"Think the jokes spoiled her appetite?" Uncle Miltie asked anxiously, as he helped Gracie clear the table.

Gracie shook her head. "She enjoyed the stories. She's under too much stress, poor dear. A little rest will do her good. How about some dessert?"

The elderly man grimaced. "Guess I also lost my appetite."

"Me, too. Why don't you get your uniform out? I'll give it a look see."

Joe returned as Uncle Miltie was climbing the stairs. "How's she doing?" Gracie asked.

Joe's face was lined with worry. "Don't know, Gracie. She's been through a lot. Not sure how much more she can handle."

Gracie patted his shoulder. "Don't worry, Joe. She's going to be okay. You'll see."

The doorbell rang. Gracie rolled her eyes and headed down the hall. Rocky Gravino was on the front step.

"Hope you don't mind my coming over unannounced?"

"No, Rocky. Of course not. Never. Come in."

She led him into the living room where Joe had settled into one of the armchairs and was absently watching a televised baseball game.

"Would you like the sound turned up?" Gracie asked.

Joe blinked. "Huh. No, that's all right, Gracie. Not really paying any attention. Oh, hello, Rocky," he added, making a move to rise.

"Don't get up, Joe," the editor replied. "How's Anna?"

Joe clenched his fists. "Not so good. Not so good."

"I'm sorry to hear that. Give her my best, would you?"

Joe nodded, but his mind was elsewhere.

Gracie steered Rocky into the kitchen where Uncle Miltie was hanging his uniform jacket on a chair back. The men exchanged greetings, then Uncle Miltie excused himself.

"Coffee?" Gracie asked.

"If it's no trouble," Rocky replied. "Taking a toll on Anna and Joe, isn't it?"

She handed him a steaming mug and carried the cookie jar to the table. The phone rang and the answering machine clicked into action. Gracie just shook her head at Rocky's inquisitive look.

"So that's why your questions about TV production, huh? It's all over town," Rocky said, taking a seat. "Paper's been swamped with calls. Everybody thinks there's a television show being shot, right this minute, in Willow Bend." He ran his fingers through his hair. "One lady said she'd seen Clint Eastwood at The Sweet Shoppe. Can you believe that? Don't know how the rumor got started, but it's already out of control."

"Poor Anna," Gracie said, running her fingers over the military jacket. "I'm really worried about her health."

"What's that?"

"Uncle Miltie's uniform. He wants to wear it tomorrow night but it's a bit small." She held it up. The band of colored medals and decorations across the breast pocket flashed in the overhead light. "I don't think letting out a couple of seams'll do the trick." She looked at her guest. "Stand up for a minute?"

Rocky raised his eyebrows but obeyed. Gracie handed him the jacket. It was too short in the arms and extremely tight across the back, but it was on.

"That's fine," she said, as Rocky slipped out of the short coat. She found her seam ripper and started to open the stitches running up the back. "This'll allow him to wear it, at least. He doesn't have to do it up, does he?"

"Nope." Rocky bit into a ginger cookie. "So, are you still feeling nervous about that Houston fellow?"

Gracie glanced up from her work. "Not sure. At least Ann McNeill's looking over the contract, so that's a relief." She ripped a couple of stitches. "I admit, I haven't the faintest notion about television or publishing, for that matter, but I don't like people being pushed. Tom Williams suggested that they might consider other agencies."

Rocky chewed. "Not a bad idea. Perhaps even run a check on our man Arnie, himself."

Gracie paused. "You could do that?"

He nodded. "Couple of phone calls to some old buddies of mine. They cover the show biz beat." Rocky reached for another cookie.

"His company's called the Houston Entertainment Agency. And Anna and Joe have until tomorrow night to make their decision."

"Oh," Rocky replied, eyeing the cookie. "Guess I'd better take this one for the road."

23

AFTER ROCKY LEFT, the men in the living room accepted Gracie's offer of decaffeinated coffee. She was just returning with an empty tray when Anna slowly crept into the kitchen and hesitantly maneuvered into a nearby chair.

Gracie was shocked by the pallor of her elderly friend's face. "Anna?" she asked, moving quickly to the women's side. "What's wrong? Are you feeling ill?"

Fat tears formed in Anna's unseeing eyes then rolled down and along the deep lines creasing her face. Gracie grabbed a few tissues and pressed them into Anna's hand. While her friend cried quietly, Gracie stood by, her hand on Anna's shoulder. The older woman was trembling. *Was she always this thin?* Gracie thought. *Oh, dear! She's losing weight. This nonsense has got to stop!*

After a couple of minutes, Anna inhaled heavily. "I'm sorry," she whispered, "for acting like a foolish old woman."

"Nonsense!" Gracie replied, plunking down in the next chair. "After what you've been through, you've every right to be upset. Why, your lives have changed dramatically in the last few days! That'd cause problems for *anyone*, believe you me." She peered into her friend's face, and noticed it was covered with a fine sheen of perspiration. "You look exhausted, dear. How about a piece of cinnamon toast and a glass of milk?"

Anna dabbed her eyes with a fresh tissue. "Don't think I could eat . . . oh, Gracie, I'm so confused! Joe and I were so pleased with the reprinting of the Lazy Lake series, and we couldn't be more thrilled and thankful to have Tom back in our lives, but . . ." She sneezed.

"Bless you."

"I don't know what to do. Mr. Houston, he . . . he seems nice, but he's so *relentless*. I . . . I know they're just children's stories . . ." Another ghost of a smile floated across her face. "It's just that I'm not sure I like what he plans to do with them. When he starts pacing and talking about them a mile a minute, I hardly recognize them." Anna stared at Gracie. The older woman's complexion was suddenly gray, her face slack.

"Please, Anna," Gracie begged. "You've got to eat something."

Anna shook her head. "And then, all those phone calls! *Everyone* wants something from me. Don't they?"

"You're not responsible for the rest of Willow Bend, Anna," Gracie replied. "Arnie Houston's contract is for you and Joe, no one else. You two must decide whether you wish to sign, and not be pressured by what others want."

The phone rang and the answering machine clicked again, silently taking another message.

"See?" Anna's face collapsed. "How can I disappoint or deny them?" She raised her head, her eyes brimming with tears. Her voice cracked, her next words were barely above a whisper. "They . . . won't get this opportunity if I . . . don't sign, will they, Gracie? Will they?"

Her arm brushed the table, sending a tissue flying. Anna reached down.

It happened so fast that Gracie barely believed her eyes. One minute, her friend was talking, the next, she was sprawled on Gracie's kitchen floor. Unconscious.

Gracie dashed to Anna's inert body and shouted for help.

THOUGH MORE THAN FIVE YEARS had passed since her dear husband Elmo had died, when Gracie eyed the inside double Emergency doors at Keefer Memorial Hospital, the raw memories roared back to her like a tidal wave. Disbelief and shock, followed by confusion, an inability to comprehend, then silence, terrible and still, as the surgeon's devastating news echoed in her brain. Fortunately, her friends had helped her through those tough, early days, and she could have asked for no son more devoted than Arlen, who himself had been grieving so.

The doors burst open. An elderly man in overalls and a weathered baseball cap lumbered through, berating the hospital staff behind him. "The town'll be ruined, I tell you. Ruined!" His right thumb was heavily bandaged.

"Mac!" Uncle Miltie exclaimed, rising with some difficulty. "What happened to you?"

Mac Medline grimaced and spun in their direction. He glanced at Gracie and flushed slightly. "Caught the darn thing in the barn door." He shook his head. "Hurts like the dickens. Hello, Gracie. Joe."

They nodded politely. Gracie thought she smelled alcohol on the local farmer's breath but, with the various hospital odors, she couldn't be certain.

"What are you all doing here?"

"Anna collapsed, but she's okay now," Joe replied. Uncle Miltie sat down. "She's a diabetic, you know."

Mac shifted his hat, revealing tufts of yellow-white hair. "Didn't. Sorry to hear she's under the weather." He paused, staring at his bandage. "Is she going to demand that the TV series be filmed here before she signs the contract? Like I hear?"

Gracie stifled a moan.

Joe shook his head. "This is exactly why she's feeling ill." He sighed. "At this moment, I wish we'd never heard of a contract or any television show."

"Best policy," Mac replied. "Forget all about it."

"Excuse me, Mac," Gracie interjected "But I believe that's for Joe and Anna to decide." Uncle Miltie nodded.

Mac's complexion darkened. "Maybe, maybe not. Whole town's at stake, you know."

"What do you mean?" Uncle Miltie asked.

Mac shoved his good hand into his dirty overalls. "Way I

see it, a Lazy Lake TV series'll be the ruination of Willow Bend. Tourist trap, USA. You folks ever been to Prince Edward Island?" They shook their heads. "Off Canada's east coast. Pretty little island. Got red soil, jim dandy for farming." He grabbed a nearby chair and straddled it. "*They* have a famous woman writer, too. Wrote books about a girl, Anne of Green Gables."

Gracie nodded. When she was young, she'd read Lucy Maud Montgomery's charming stories about a red-haired, high-spirited orphan. Gracie was always partial to Anne's spunky nature and, of course, hair color.

"Well, that's all you see now. Anne this, Anne that. Every shop sells red-headed dolls and Green Gables doll houses. It's like there's nothin' else. Like I said, the island's pretty-near perfect for farming. There's fishing, too—you outta go to a lobster dinner. My word! Those folks know how to put on a spread—even horse racing. But do you think they advertise any of that?" He vehemently shook his head. "They've got a bridge to the island now. Folks call it Anne's Span, believe it or not."

"Nobody's talking about anything like that," Joe said.

Mac ripped his cap off his head and ruffled a few wispy strands. "Mebbe not now. But give it some time. I warn ya. It'll ruin Willow Bend. Just the way, it's ruined P.E.I. Why, that freckled kid's been on their license plate, for Pete's sake! Is that what you and Anna want for Willow Bend?"

"Of course not," Joe replied, rising to his feet.

Mac stood as well.

"Wait a minute," Uncle Miltie said, hoisting himself up.

"Well, if your wife demands—"

"My wife will do whatever she wants."

"I'm warning you."

"Hold on, guys," Uncle Miltie said. "This's no—"

Mac was pointing his index finger directly at Joe's chest. "I'm not going to let it happen, Joe. I'm telling you."

"Don't threaten me!" Joe replied, his voice rising.

The doors flew open again and a tall man covered in green scrubs approached the group. "What's going on, here?" he demanded. "This is a hospital, gentlemen! You've got problems, take them outside." He looked at Mac. "Still here, Mr. Medline? Would you like an escort to your car? Perhaps have someone drive you home?"

"Don't be ridiculous!" Mac snapped, turning toward the exit. As the automatic doors swung opened, he twisted his neck. "Nobody's going to turn Willow Bend into a circus. Hear that, Joe? Nobody."

The doors *whooshed* shut. Gracie released a sigh of relief.

The physician smiled briefly. "Got a bee in his bonnet, doesn't he? Now, which one of you men is Mr. Searfoss?"

Joe squeezed Gracie's hand and nodded. "I am. Is Anna all right?"

"I'm Dr. Natalie. Your wife experienced insulin shock and low blood pressure. But she's fine now."

Thank You, Lord! Gracie thought.

"That glass of orange juice you gave her was the right thing to do. I'd like to keep her overnight, though, to monitor her insulin levels." His green eyes narrowed. "She's under a lot of stress, Mr. Searfoss. She told me about the fire. Awfully sorry, sir." Joe nodded his thanks. "Your wife says she's not been sleeping. Obviously not eating enough. *Very* unhealthy, you know that. We've got to try and maintain those blood sugar levels. I suggest you find a way to reduce her stress or she'll be in here again." He clapped Joe on the shoulder. "We don't want that, do we?"

Joe shook his head. "May I see her?"

"For a few minutes. I've given her a little something to help her sleep."

"You go ahead," Gracie said. "Uncle Miltie and I will wait here. Give her our love. And thank you, Peter," she added, addressing the doctor.

"Poor old girl," Uncle Miltie said. "Hardly got the chance to enjoy her good news."

"Well, we've got our marching orders, now. Don't we?"

He nodded, fiddling with a pamphlet. "Circle-the-wagons time."

"What's wrong with Mac?"

Her uncle shrugged. "Hasn't been the same since the death

of his wife. I heard he'd had a rough year, lost some crops, but I didn't know he was this upset." He banged a piece of paper against his leg.

"What's that?"

He stared at his hands, as though surprised they held something. "Oh, some brochure on diabetes." He handed it to Gracie. "Was just reading it to pass the time."

She leafed through the four-part pullout. One page was devoted to a list of symptoms that suggested a possible diagnosis of diabetes. She recalled them from discussions with Anna. Gracie folded it up and handed it back. Uncle Miltie slid it onto a nearby table.

"What are you two doing here?" a woman's voice exclaimed.

Gracie spun around to see her friend Nancy Bixler approaching. Nancy and Uncle Miltie exchanged hellos. Gracie explained the situation to the nurse.

"Dear Anna," Nancy said. "Diabetes can be problematic. She staying overnight?"

Gracie nodded.

"Just as well. Better safe than sorry." Nancy paused. "Any chance you'd give me that walnut squares recipe from the shower? I made the mistake of telling Fred about it and he keeps asking when I'm going to make them."

"Of course," Gracie replied. "I'll send you a copy. How are Phyllis and Darren doing? He sure is a cutie."

Nancy smiled. "A real sweetheart. Funny you should ask. Just had Phyllis in about an hour ago. No, no, the baby's fine. It was her daughter, Kate. Nasty fall off her bike, poor thing. Nothing serious, but we X-rayed just in case."

Gracie shook her head. "Thank heavens, she's all right. She does get around on that bike of hers. She was almost hit by a car outside my house the other day."

It was Nancy's turn to shake her head. "Hasn't learned her lesson, that's for sure. She's a funny one."

"How do you mean?" Uncle Miltie asked.

Nancy hesitated. "Well, demanding a lot of attention for one thing. "Of course, that's natural. She's used to being an only child and *poof!* someone new, cuddly and very vulnerable and demanding arrives. But . . . it's not just that. She's, well, *secretive*. Wouldn't explain the accident." The nurse laughed lightly. "Well, I've forgotten what it was like to be her age, and it's been years since my kids were eleven, so maybe I'm reading too much between the lines." A disembodied voice crackled through the overhead speakers. She shrugged. "I'd love to stay and chat but duty calls. I'll check in on Anna."

Joe arrived a couple of minutes later and told them that Anna was resting comfortably and sent her regards.

"Is there anything she needs?" Gracie asked, as they stepped into the warm night air.

"Uh huh. A few juice boxes. Doctor says she should be carrying one with her at all times."

They climbed into Fannie Mae.

"I'll pick them up tomorrow, first thing," Gracie said, turning the key.

"She keeps asking me what we should do," Joe said, shaking his head as the Cadillac purred through the night. "I don't know what to say. Tom's been encouraging us to think on it. Take our time."

"It's not easy," Uncle Miltie said from the back seat. "Used to be a simple question of whether you and Anna wanted to let that Arnie fellow market her stories. But now . . . now, it involves the whole town, doesn't it?"

"Seems to," Joe replied wearily. "What's the right answer?"

"I wish I knew," Gracie said, turning a corner.

They drove in silence for a few blocks. Gracie glanced in her rear view mirror. Uncle Miltie was fast asleep. She looked across at Joe. Eyes closed, his chin was touching his chest.

Dear Lord, she prayed silently, *thank You for giving Anna a second chance. With Your support, I promise to do a better job to protect her and Joe. Please, help me to know how to guide and advise them. I'm not always sure what's best so I will listen hard for Your voice. You've put a lot on their plate lately, but I hope, with my love and care, and that of Uncle Miltie and their other friends, it won't prove to be too much.*

Gracie turned into her driveway. As she shut off the engine, another thought popped into her mind. *Please, God, watch over Mac Medline and help him find contentment. He seemed so full of anger and fear, I'm worried that he will do something foolish, perhaps, even dangerous. Guide him. Amen.*

A silver streak from the moon arched over her garden patch, reminding her of her mother's old garden saying about planting rows of lettuce: *Lettuce be faithful, Lettuce be kind, Lettuce be obedient, Lettuce really love one another.*

Gracie glanced at the sleeping men and silently planted another one: *Lettuce pray and give thanks to our precious Lord. Amen.*

25

GRACIE ROSE EARLY on Tuesday. While praise-walking in the morning light with Gooseberry, she mentally ran through the final catering preparations necessary for the evening's memorial display event. She always found the rhythm and movement of her body conducive to thinking. By concentrating on her stride and breathing and admiring the leafy streets and curving paths of the town she loved, her thoughts roamed freely, often revealing something important. A tidbit or connection that she couldn't remember or put together during the regular bustle of her life. This morning, however, nothing dramatic jumped into her head while she admired the peonies, tulips and other late spring flowers dotting the gardens of Willow Bend. She didn't mind. She had already been greatly rewarded by the restoration of Anna's health.

Marge had offered to bake four deep-dish apricot pies,

using dried apricots. After discussing recipes, they had agreed on the addition of both grated orange and lemon peel as well as a handful of raisins.

As Gracie pounded through Julius Norton Fairweather Park, Gooseberry darted ahead and leapt onto part of the colorful children's play structure. Gracie couldn't help laughing out loud as she watched her big orange tomcat, the tip of his plumed tail still charred black, slip nimbly up the bright-blue ladder and into the barrel tunnel. She waved to a man nearby walking a large black dog. As she completed her circuit around the play structure, Goose's head popped out the other side of the tunnel. She called to him and turned, gearing up for the return home.

Instead of jumping down and joining her, Gooseberry meowed loudly. Gracie pulled up short, wheeled, and marched toward the wild, green eyes. The barrel tunnel was connected to a bright yellow slide. Her cat stood precariously on the edge, one white paw reaching tentatively along the slippery chute. "Come on, Goosie," she encouraged, standing in sand at the bottom of the slide. "You can do it."

His cry of frustration deepened.

"Okay, then, Mr. Adventurer. Turn around and I'll meet you on the other side." She dutifully walked over to the ladder, damp sand trickling into her shoes, to find her cat perched on the top step. "Well? Come on. Jump."

Gooseberry's back arched and he shifted from side to side.

"Oh, for heaven's sake, Goosie!" She moved alongside the ladder and held out her arms. "Come here, then."

Poised to jump, Gooseberry suddenly froze at the nearby sound of barking. The black dog lunged at the ladder. With a squeal, Gooseberry spun and flew back through the tunnel. Before she could react, Gracie heard a startled cry and then the sound of nails scratching against plastic. She dashed a couple of steps to see her normally haughty feline slithering down the slide, white paws desperately grasping at the slick banana-yellow surface. Then, with a sudden *plop*, Gooseberry landed unceremoniously, feet first, in the sand.

The owner of the dog shouted his apologies and dragged his unruly beast away. Two other men on the far side of the park, previously engrossed in conversation, glanced up. The shorter one seemed to be shouting.

Gracie was shaking so hard trying not to laugh, she collapsed on the slide. For a moment, she thought one of the men was Tom Williams and waved. The figure turned quickly away. Gracie stared, now watching the second man. He was shorter, younger by the looks of his movements, very energetic. The early sunlight was dazzling, so Gracie wouldn't have sworn to it, but she thought the second man resembled Arnie Houston. Having her glasses might have helped.

Gooseberry meowed loudly. Then, he rose to his full

height of twelve inches, stretched luxuriously, swept his head away from her, and daintily minced out of the sand.

Gracie couldn't contain herself. In a burst, laughter exploded from her throat. Then, she felt herself moving, and tried to grab hold of the edges of the slide. But it was too late. She slid rapidly to the bottom. With a heavy *thud*, Gracie Parks dropped to the sand like a stone, her breath flying from her lungs like a frightened bird.

Embarrassed, she glanced up, trying to regain her breath. The two men had disappeared. She saw Gooseberry's striped tail flicking mischievously as he strolled sedately from the park. Despite her bruised dignity, Gracie giggled.

Upon her return, Gracie hastily showered and changed, then fed a still disdainful Gooseberry. But after a couple of nibbles, the big cat arched his back and welcomed her soft stroking. She made a quick call to the hospital and was delighted to learn that Anna's night had been restful. Then, she put in a call to Marge.

"On schedule," her best friend replied cheerfully. "Just rolling more dough."

Gracie relayed the news about Anna.

"Poor thing!" Marge replied. "I didn't realize. When'll she be coming home?"

"I've no idea."

"Such a shame! Is Joe all right?"

"He's fine. Spending a lot of time with Uncle Miltie."

"That's nice. Uh, Gracie? That nephew of Anna's, he single?"

Gracie sighed. Sadly, Marge's last husband hadn't been a keeper. It meant she had ever since kept an alert eye on the entire segment of the world's population comprised of eligible males, no matter what their age.

"I believe so." She heard a loud bang. "Everything all right?"

"Uh huh. Just dropped the rolling pin, is all. You going to invite him to the seniors center event?"

Gracie was flipping on her oven. "Sorry, who?"

"Tom. Is he coming tonight?"

"I'm not sure, but I'll extend an invitation."

"Would you? That'd be lovely. Aren't too many interesting new men around Willow Bend. Got to take care of the ones who do."

Gracie knew that Marge would prattle on, so she cut in. "Sorry but I've got to go. Check in with you later, okay?" She hung up the phone, made a pot of coffee then began mixing a quadruple batch of her very special brownies. She was just pouring warm fudge sauce over two large, square pans of batter when Uncle Miltie and Joe entered the kitchen. "Sleep well?"

They both nodded and Uncle Miltie kissed her on the check. She told Joe about her call to the hospital. "Thank

God," he replied, his eyes shining with tears. "She really is quite something, don't you think?"

Gracie and Uncle Miltie agreed heartily.

"Smells good," Uncle Miltie said, peering over her shoulder. He reached into a large bowl and swiped a finger full of fudge sauce. "*Umm.*"

She playfully slapped his hand. "That's for later. Coffee's ready. Cereal and fruit are on the table. Also, some fresh multi-grain bread and plum jelly for toast. I'll join you in a jiffy." She poured the remaining batter over the fudge sauce and gently slid the pans into the oven.

Uncle Miltie poured three cups of coffee, offered one to Gracie and to Joe, then carried his own to the table. Joe grabbed the cream and sugar. In a couple of minutes, they were munching cereal and spreading rose-colored jelly on toast.

"Busy day, huh, Gracie?" her uncle said.

She nodded, her mouth filled with bananas, milk and granola.

"Me, too," he continued. "I'll be heading to the center around noon. Have a bite to eat, do a little clearing up. You coming with me, Joe?"

"Are you going to visit Anna?" Joe asked, grabbing a slice of toast as it popped up.

"I was thinking about mid-morning. That'd give me a chance to get all my baking done. Want to come along?"

Joe glanced at Uncle Miltie. "Would that be all right? I'd like to spend some time with her. I could meet you later at the center."

"Fine."

His expression became serious. "I don't really like doing this, but you're our dearest friends." Gracie and her uncle exchanged a puzzled glance. "I know we really shouldn't be asking either of you for any more favors," Joe continued, "but there's one more thing we'd like to request of you."

"Anything," Gracie replied. "You know that, Joe." Uncle Miltie nodded.

"Thank you . . . well, here goes: We'd like both of you to witness our new wills."

Both Gracie and her uncle were stunned into silence. Uncle Miltie found his tongue first. "Witness your . . . wills?"

Oh, no, Gracie thought. *I'm not sure I'm happy about where this is headed.*

Joe leaned forward. "Ever since Tom arrived, Anna and I've talked about getting around to it, but after Anna's collapse, she asked me to have Ann McNeill revise them as soon as possible." He hesitated. "She's afraid . . . something's going to happen to her."

"Nothing's going to happen to her!" Gracie replied. "She'll be home soon, right as rain."

Joe gave her an appreciative smile. "I think so too, but she's worried and she's got her mind made up. You see, now

171

that the books are being reprinted, Anna feels she has a legacy to pass on. We didn't have anyone to will it to before our nephew showed up but now . . ."

"Now?" Gracie asked.

"Now, we'd like to leave our estates to Tom." Joe looked a little sheepish. "Mine's not much, bit of life insurance, but Anna's could be, what with the books and maybe even television royalties." One after the other, Joe looked his friends in the eyes. "Will you?"

"Of course," they replied simultaneously.

Relief flooded across Joe Searfoss's lined face. "I knew I could count on you. Of course, we'll tell Tom when the time's right."

The phone rang. Gracie excused herself. "Yes? Oh, hello, Ann. Yes, Joe's right here." She turned, covering the mouthpiece with her palm. "It's Ann McNeill, Joe."

His jaw dropped. "With Anna's collapse, I'd forgotten all about calling her. What'm I going to say?"

"Have you and Anna made a decision?" Uncle Miltie asked.

Joe wearily shook his head. "Like I said last night at the hospital, wish I'd never heard of the darn thing."

"How about I tell her you'll give her a call a bit later, okay?"

Joe nodded gratefully. Gracie spoke quickly over the phone then listened for a couple of minutes before hanging up. "No problem," she said. "Ann's afternoon is pretty open. There is one thing she asked me to tell you immediately, though." Joe eyed her carefully. "She thinks the contract's somewhat one-sided."

Joe pulled a hand across his heavy-lidded eyes. "What's that mean?"

"She wouldn't recommend you signing it, as is. Seems Mr. Houston's asking for a lot more than is standard."

Joe closed his eyes.

Uncle Miltie patted his friend's arm. "Don't worry, Joe. It'll work out. Once we get Anna home safe and sound, things will be better. You'll see."

"I hope you're right, Uncle Miltie. I really hope you're right."

While Uncle Miltie and Joe cleared the table and shared the dish duty, Gracie sifted the dry ingredients for a double batch of the hot milk sponge cake, then beat the eggs. She added the sugar and lemon juice, then carefully folded in the dry ingredients. She pulled the mug containing hot milk from the microwave, poured it into the mixture then blended it quickly. As the men wiped the table and free counter space, Gracie filled four lightly greased layer pans and set them aside. Opening the oven, she tested the brownies and removed them to cool. She carefully pushed the layer pans into the oven and reset the timer.

The men washed and dried the last two bowls. "You're

hired!" she said, glancing admiringly around at her neat and tidy kitchen. "It makes *such* a difference to have a clean-up crew. I can't thank you enough."

"No thanks necessary," Joe said, wiping his hands. "Least I can do to show my appreciation for your wonderful hospitality and friendship."

"Me, too," said her uncle.

She gave them both a quick hug. "Why don't you two take a break? The cakes'll be ready in about fifteen minutes. We can leave for the hospital shortly after."

"Come on, Joe. You can help me load some boxes into the car."

Gracie smiled as she watched the elderly pair working together. She was thrilled to see how both their attitudes and self-confidence improved when they were completing a task. Especially one that was near and dear to their hearts, like planning for the veterans' memorial display. It reminded her how valuable and healthy it was to every human being to feel useful and needed. She wondered if Mac Medline had recently experienced such simple joy and satisfaction. Then she prayed that he had.

26

GRACIE, WHAT DO YOU THINK we should do?" Anna asked later that morning, as Joe left the hospital room to get coffee. "I've prayed all night for an answer but nothing comes." She sniffled. "I . . . I think the Lord's angry at me."

Gracie examined her friend with rising concern. Anna's face still looked drawn and tired. Of course, it didn't help that she was lying, almost lost in crisp white sheets, in a hospital bed. "Nonsense! Of course, He's not mad at you, Anna!" she replied, squeezing Anna's frail wrist. "You've done nothing wrong."

A tear streamed down Anna's pale cheek. "I never wanted to cause trouble. Do you think He's testing me, Gracie? Like He tested His son, Jesus Christ, in the wilderness? Tempting

Joe and me with the possibility of wealth and seeing if we would succumb and worship false gods?"

Gracie didn't know what to say, but she knew Anna needed to talk so she remained quiet and listened with all her might.

Anna clenched her fists. "Oh, I just don't know. He's blessed us, especially with Tommy's return." For a moment, her face brightened. "He came to visit last night. Poor boy, he was in quite a state! So worried about Joe and me. Tommy talked for a long time about how tough the television business is. He said they're all selfish and will do almost anything to make money. That Joe and I were vulnerable, that I had to be very careful or they'd change my stories to suit their needs, and that Mr. Houston will take advantage of us. That was frightening enough but . . . there was something else." She hesitated.

"What, dear?"

"Tommy, himself. He kept starting to say something then stopped. I asked him what it was, but he just shrugged it off. Said nothing was more important than my health. That's so considerate, but I can't help worrying." Her fingers pulled on the bed sheet, and the extra juice boxes Gracie had brought tumbled to the floor. "Oh, dear! I'm sorry."

Gracie patted her hand, quickly picked up the boxes, and put them on a nearby table.

"You know," Anna was saying, "I've thought about the

contract every which way. When everyone seemed so eager to have the television series filmed here, Joe and I felt perhaps I shouldn't sign with Mr. Houston unless he agreed. *That* was what the Lord wanted us to do . . . but now." Her voice broke. "It's even worse. I . . . I heard Mac shouting last night and . . . later, one of the nurses told me what he said."

She slumped back on the pillow, suddenly exhausted. "I'm so confused. My own town is divided because of my books. So much has happened. I never asked for any of it. Well, maybe I said a few prayers for the safety of our future, you know, but *nothing* like this! And our home . . . we can't keep relying on your hospitality. You've been more than kind but we've got to go." Her voice rose. "Oh, Gracie, what am I going to do? Mr. Houston wants an answer today! What *am* I going to do?"

Gracie's heart went out to her friend. Though she didn't know the answer, she knew who did. "There, there," Gracie replied, hugging her nearly hysterical friend. "It's going to be all right." After a couple of minutes, Anna's sobbing diminished.

Gracie leaned back and spoke slowly. "I don't have all the answers, but I'll tell you this: please, stop worrying about staying with Uncle Miltie and me. I sincerely mean it, Anna. You're no trouble and we *love* your company. Okay?" Anna was silent, then nodded. "Good. Now, as to Mr. Houston . . . why don't we pray together? Sometimes, it's just hard to hear what the Lord's trying to tell us. Remember what Pastor Paul preached last week: The Lord will overshadow you, and you will find refuge under His wings."

"Amen," Anna whispered.

The two women clasped their hands, bowed their heads, and prayed silently for guidance. *Dear God,* Gracie began, *I know You're busy and have lots of demands, but please help my dear friend, Anna, and her husband, Joe. You have blessed them with new opportunities, now they need Your support as to how to best use Your gifts. I know You didn't mean to upset Anna, and I'm sure You know her health and physical limitations but, Lord, if this is some test of Anna and Joe's faith, I think You've seen the answer.*

She glanced up. Eyes closed, Anna Searfoss's hands were on her stomach, her head sunk into the pillow. Gracie smiled softly. "Sweet dreams," she whispered.

Gracie left Joe at the hospital, then nipped into the Willow Mart for a couple of pounds of butter before steering Fannie Mae home for lunch. As she pulled open the screen door, she heard a women's voice followed by the sound of her coffee grinder. Phyllis Nickolson and her daughter were sitting at the kitchen table. Darren was sleeping in a car seat resting on the table, near his mother. The open cookie jar sat beside Katie.

"Oh, hello, Phyllis!" Gracie said, dropping the butter on the counter. "And Katie." The young girl ignored her, her attention fixed on a large bandage covering her knee. A half-eaten cookie lay on a plate in front of her. Gracie approached the car seat and stroked the sleeping baby's chin. "And little Darren!" she said, lowering her voice. "How nice to see you all."

"Thanks for whispering, but," Phyllis replied, her freckled face breaking into a tired smile, "for once, he seems to be sleeping like a log."

"Phyllis and I were just about to start a pot of coffee," Uncle Miltie said, standing at the counter, a spray of ground coffee dusting his hands and the nearby counter.

"Perfect timing," Gracie replied. "We'll have it brewing in a jiffy."

"I'm sorry," Phyllis said. "We really shouldn't have come unannounced. It's just that I was taking Katie—she's got the afternoon off, you see, professional development day at the school—and Darren to the library. Thought we'd drop by to say hello."

"And I'm so glad you did," Gracie said. "I was dying for a good cup of coffee."

Her phone rang. Gracie excused herself and picked up the receiver. It was Arnie Houston asking for Anna.

"I'm sorry, Mr. Houston, but she's in the hospital." Gracie heard him take a sharp intake of breath but wasn't sure if it was from shock or from taking a fast drag on one of his cigarettes.

"Hospital! Are you kidding?"

"Of course not."

"Oh, man," he moaned. "This is a disaster. Is she all right?"

"She's going to be fine."

"Well, I need to see her, Mrs. Parks. What's the name of the hospital and her room number?"

Gracie paused. She knew that Houston could easily look the hospital up in the phone book, call and get the information. "Anna needs rest, Mr. Houston. She's not seeing anyone but family and close friends. Doctor's orders."

"She'll see me," he crowed. "What hospital?"

Warning him again about Anna's fragile condition, Gracie reluctantly gave him the name.

As she hung up, she apologized to Phyllis and quickly called Keefer Memorial.

"Nurse Bixler, please."

Phyllis Nickolson raised her eyebrows realizing Gracie was phoning her place of work.

After a while, a woman's voice came on the phone. "Hello?"

"Oh, Nancy, I'm so glad I caught you! It's Gracie."

"Are you all right?" the nurse asked. "Your voice sounds funny."

"I'm fine. Just worried about Anna. A man by the name of Arnie Houston is going to try and visit her. Is there any chance you can refuse to let him?"

"Well," Nancy said. "That's a trifle unusual, but I'll try and help. What's the situation?"

"It's a long story, but he's part of the reason she's in there. I'm afraid if he talks to her, she'll have a relapse."

"*Umm.* Let me check her chart." There was a rustling noise. "Got it. Well, she did have a rough night. I suppose I could make a notation to restrict her visitors to family."

"Would you? I don't want you to get into any trouble—"

"No trouble," Nancy replied. "Anything for the benefit of the patient, that's our motto."

Gracie thanked her and hung up.

"What was *that* about?" Phyllis asked.

Uncle Miltie glanced at his niece. Gracie hesitated.

Phyllis lifted her hands. "That's all right. None of my business."

"How about that cup of java?" Uncle Miltie asked.

As the coffee dripped, Phyllis chatted about settling Darren and the rest of the Nickolson household into a routine. They laughed when she said she'd forgotten how loud a baby's cry can be in the middle of the night. "Haven't figured out the difference between 'I'm hungry' and 'I'm wet.'"

"It's impossible to sleep," Katie said, her braces glinting. "I told you, Mrs. Parks. He cries all the time."

"Now, Katie," her mom started, "we've discussed this. Remember, he's just a baby. He can't talk like you and me. Crying's his only way of communicating."

Katie picked at her bandage. "Well, he *communicates* an awful lot."

Gracie and Uncle Miltie exchanged grins.

Phyllis sighed and gave Gracie a look that said: *Can we talk?*

Uncle Miltie winked.

Gracie rose. "You've got to see this new recipe I found for baked fried chicken," she said, gesturing for Phyllis to follow her to the kitchen counter.

"I'd love to," her guest replied, joining her. While Gracie flipped through the pages of an oversized cookbook, Phyllis whispered her thanks for having Arnie Houston call. He'd been very apologetic, she said, and had offered to pay for any damages to Katie's bike. Fortunately, there were none.

"Back in a minute," said Uncle Miltie. Half a minute later, he returned, his uniform jacket in hand.

"Look at it this, Katie. It's my uniform from the Second World War. You heard of the war?"

"Uh huh," the girl replied, banging her good leg against the table.

"Katie," her mom warned. "Please. Darren's sleeping."

As Uncle Miltie explained the colorful row of medals and ribbons decorating his jacket, Phyllis continued to whisper to Gracie. "Not sure what to do with her, Gracie. She's acting out, runs around the house screaming. Her teachers say she's causing problems in class. I know she's looking for more attention but . . ." she drew a breath. "It's so hard with the baby."

Gracie nodded.

"I . . . I was hoping you could help."

Uh oh, Gracie thought, collecting her thoughts. There was no way she could baby-sit today, not with the seniors center event. "Uh . . . yes?"

"I know it's an awful imposition. And I wouldn't ask if I wasn't desperate but . . . d'you think you could ask Anna if Katie could be considered for a role in her TV series?"

Gracie blinked. This wasn't at all what she had expected. "I don't know," she replied, when she found her voice. "There really isn't any show at the moment."

"Oh," Phyllis said, her face falling. "Everyone's talking about it. Someone even said Steven Spielberg was in town, scouting locations. I just thought . . ." She glanced at Katie. "Leave that bandage alone, young lady! It'll never heal if you keep picking at it," she snapped, then flushed darkly. "I'm sorry, honey." Darren began to cry. "Oh, dear," Phyllis moaned, moving to her infant son.

"Come here, Katie," Gracie said, approaching the girl. "Let's take a look at that. I haven't changed a bandage on a pretty little girl in a long time. How about you come with me and we put on a fresh one, okay? Then Uncle Miltie will make you an ice cream sundae. How's that sound?" She glanced at Phyllis for approval. Katie's mother nodded thankfully.

The girl licked her lips. "I like chocolate."

"Is there anything else?" Uncle Miltie agreed happily.

In the washroom, as she gently removed the bandage and then the gauze dressing covering much of Katie's knee, Gracie asked her how she fell.

The girl shifted on the toilet seat and tugged at her pigtails.

"You sure like riding your bike, don't you? You go any place in particular?"

Again no answer.

So much for that, Miss Marple, Gracie thought, changing tactics. "Your mom tells me you'd like to be an actress."

Katie's little face lit up. "I've been in school plays, you know. I was the star. Ouch, that hurts!"

"Sorry, dear," Gracie said, dabbing topical ointment around the scratches.

"My mom says Mrs. Searfoss'll give me a part. I can't wait." She clapped her hands. "She says I'll get to wear period costumes and a hat."

As Gracie rebandaged the injury, she replied, "I'm not sure it's Mrs. Searfoss's decision."

The girl began bouncing. "My mom said I'll get a part."

"I know she did, dear." She paused for a moment. How to

tell the child the truth without implying that her mother lied? "It's just that your mom was . . . misinformed. Nothing's been decided yet."

"I want it. I want it. She said I could have it." Katie chewed her lip for a moment. "She loves *him* more'n me."

"Who, dear?"

She jabbed a finger toward the kitchen. "Him!"

Gracie shook her head and held the girl's hands. They felt small and lost in her own. "Of course, she doesn't. You know that. She loves you both." She began putting away the medical kit. "You're a big girl, Katie. Your mom needs your help now."

Katie crossed her arms. "I don't care what she needs! I didn't ask for a brother. I hate him! I *hate* him!"

Gracie grabbed the little girl and hugged her. "No, you don't. You're just upset, I understand. But hating is wrong. You know that, Katie. You also know that your mom and dad and God love you very much."

"But I want to be an actress," cried the girl, her voice muffled. "Can you ask Mrs. Searfoss for me?"

"I told you, honey. She's not the one who's making the decision."

The girl reared back, her tiny face marred with tears. "Then who is? Please, if you tell me who is, I'll be good as gold. You'll see. I promise. Please tell me."

Gracie hesitated but the girl's expression was so desperate, she gave in. She didn't like to deny the child. *And really,* she asked herself, *what would be the harm in telling her?* Katie would never be able to act on it. "I think Mr. Houston—you remember him?"

The girl sniffled. "The man who ran me over?"

"*Almost* ran you over, remember. Yes. I think he might know."

27

UPON THEIR RETURN to the kitchen, Katie spied a bowl of chocolate ice cream covered with chocolate sauce and a dollop of whipped cream. As her mother and Uncle Miltie watched with delight, the pigtailed girl flew to the table, grabbed a spoon and dove in.

"Wait a minute, young lady," Phyllis said. "You thank Uncle Miltie and Mrs. Parks."

The spoon hesitated just long enough for Katie to gasp a thank you.

Uncle Miltie watched the spoon fly and chuckled. "Got a hollow leg, that one."

Phyllis adjusted the pacifier resting on Darren's blue jumpsuit. The baby's eyes remained shut, his breathing regular.

Gracie heard a familiar noise, turned and opened the

screen door. Gooseberry strode in, meowing a greeting. "Hello, Goosie," she said. Ignoring her, he marched immediately to his bowl, in case something had appeared since his breakfast. Finding nothing, he spun, flopped onto his bottom, and began washing his front paws.

The baby burped. Gooseberry's head shot up. Instantly on his feet, he trotted to the table, winding his way through Gracie's and then Uncle Miltie's legs. Abandoning her half-eaten sundae, Katie jumped up and dashed over to her mother.

The cat hesitated, ears alert.

"Let's go, Mom," the girl demanded, tugging Phyllis's arm. "I want to go *now*."

"Katie, darling, stop!" Her mother looked at her daughter in astonishment. "What's gotten into you? You haven't even finished your ice cream. Now, be a good girl and sit back down."

"Goosie, Goosie," Gracie purred. "He *loves* little girls. Come on, Goosie. Come see Katie."

"No," Katie replied, yanking harder. She grabbed one of the baby bags. "Let's go!"

The baby gurgled.

Gooseberry froze, green eyes staring at the little girl. Suddenly, he hissed and arched his back. Katie shrieked.

Horrified, Gracie cried, "Gooseberry!"

Darren wailed. Katie dropped the baby bag, almost flattening the cat, and raced out the screen door.

"Katie!" Phyllis shouted, over the din caused by her weeping baby. "Katie, come back!"

"I'll get her," Gracie said, on her way out. "You handle Darren."

She found the girl, arms crossed, on the front porch swing. "Are you all right?" Gracie asked.

Katie nodded. "I want to ride my bike."

"There'll be no riding that bike for a week!" her mother's voice snapped. With the car seat containing her noisy infant in one hand, Phyllis Nickolson stepped onto the porch. She marched over to the girl and raised her voice over Darren's angry cries. "Now, you apologize to Mrs. Parks, then you get right back in there and put your bowl in the sink. After that, straight to the car. You hear me?"

Uncle Miltie had quietly moved onto the porch, baby bags slung over his shoulder. Katie nodded, mumbled what might have been an apology, then stalked back into the kitchen. A moment later, the screen door banged again. Katie skipped to the car, jumped into the backseat, and slammed the door.

Gracie exhaled quietly. With the baby's wailing and the tension between mother and daughter, she was on edge. *Whew!* she thought. *Raising kids seems a lot tougher than it used to.*

"I'm terribly sorry about Gooseberry," she said, as

Darren's cries subsided. "He's never done anything like that before."

Phyllis slipped the pacifier into her son's mouth. "No need," she replied, her voice uneven.

Gracie could sense the strain the new mother was under and felt helpless.

"Sometimes babies and cats aren't a good mix." Phyllis shifted the car seat to the other hand then sighed heavily. "I just don't know what I'm going to do about that girl."

Gracie considered saying something like "You need to give her a little time," but it seemed too trite and too easy, coming from someone whose own child was grown up. Instead, she astounded herself by saying, "I'll see what I can do about Katie and a television part. Can't promise anything but..."

Her friend's eyes lit up. "Would you?" She grasped Gracie with her free hand. "I'd be so grateful. Anything. *Anything* to take her mind off ... to give her some confidence."

Uncle Miltie and Gracie escorted Phyllis and the now-slumbering infant to the car. As her friend carefully strapped in Darren, Gracie thought about her own time as a new mother. For one thing, there had been no fancy car seats in those days; hardly anyone even wore a seat belt! Though she and Elmo had hoped for more children, for some reason, known solely to Him, God had blessed them with just one. Now, as she watched the Nickolson family drive off, she wondered. Had she been fortunate enough to have more children, would she have coped any better than Phyllis?

She waved, thankful she didn't have to find out. "Come on, Uncle Miltie," she said. "That ice cream sundae looked mighty good."

28

HALF AN HOUR LATER, Gracie poked the tub of ice cream and leaned back. With a dramatic flourish, Uncle Miltie dropped his spoon into his empty bowl.

"My kind of lunch," the elderly man stated.

Gracie smiled, rose and popped the ice cream into the freezer. "Think I'm going to go for another walk. Heaven knows, after *that* many calories, I need a bit of exercise."

"All set for tonight?" her uncle asked, carrying their bowls to the sink.

She nodded, quickly washing the few dishes and placing them on the rack to dry. "Just have to ice the brownies. We'll make the punch and cut everything up when we get there. Makes it a lot easier with the center having its own kitchen with coffee and tea pots, cups and saucers. You ready?" She glanced at the kitchen clock: 1:55 P.M.

"Uh huh. Joe and I've loaded the trunk already. Still room for the food, though."

"Not to worry. There's room in Marge's car. Well," she added, draping the dish cloth over the faucet. "I'll be back by four-thirty. Marge's coming by 'round five. We'll pack up and leave about five-thirty, okay?"

"Peachy," he replied, heading for the living room. "Think I'll go and catch up on the world news. Might be missing something. Have a good walk, dear."

Gooseberry was nowhere to be found. It was probably better that way since Gracie wanted a word or two with him about his unacceptable behavior. So, slinging her purse over her shoulder, she set out on her own. Initially, she just hummed "I Stand Amazed," enjoying the rhythm of her stride and the warmth of the air along her neck. Inevitably, her thoughts shifted to tackling the schedule for the evening. This was one of her simpler catering events. No sit-down meals or fancy preparations required. Pretty easy, actually, she told herself, ticking the tasks off as she slid her hand along a picket fence: ice the brownies, cut all the desserts—in the smaller sizes appreciated by older appetites—mix the punch, brew both coffee and tea, lay out the cutlery, napkins and dishes—napkins! Her hand flew to her mouth. She'd completely forgotten to pick some up. For a moment, she stood stock still, in the middle of the sidewalk. Then, she quickly reached in the fannypack she'd strapped on for her cell phone, and poked in the number for Marge Lawrence's gift shop.

When her best friend answered, Gracie explained the emergency.

"No *problemo*," Marge replied cheerily. "Remember the Rotary Dinner?"

Gracie grimaced and rounded a corner. A last-minute fill-in job as a favor to Rocky Gravino. "How could I forget?" she replied, her breath coming in gasps.

Marge chuckled. "Not easy when you're almost poisoned. Well, there were lots of napkins left over. With all the excitement, I just grabbed them during clean-up. They're in my pantry. Say, I can hear traffic. Where are you?"

Gracie pictured the bold red, white and blue striped pattern of the leftover napkins. "Never mind. They'd be perfect! Very patriotic. Could you bring them?"

"You'll never guess who just dropped by."

Marge's tone was a dead giveaway. "Tom Williams?"

"The very same. Shopping for Anna. Isn't that the sweetest thing? I knew just the item for her. Remember those new English scented soaps I've been telling you about?"

Gracie murmured something.

"In the end, he bought four." She paused for a moment, then Gracie heard her speaking to someone else. "Gracie? Sorry, a customer. As I was saying, Tom and I had a lovely chat. Says he's really enjoying Willow Bend. Might even settle down here one day."

"Is that so?" Gracie replied, picking up her pace.

"He seems like such a nice man. Asked me all kinds of questions about Joe and Anna. Said he wants to know everything about them. Isn't that the sweetest thing?" she repeated.

"Very." Gracie slowed her stride, her mind suddenly occupied with thoughts of Tom Williams. The stranger continued to be a puzzle. Though she didn't like to think it, Gracie realized there was another way to look at his behavior. After all, he could just have easily been *learning* about the Searfosses so that he would seem more knowledgeable when they were together. Her mind spun further. If that were the case, maybe Tom *had* been with Arnie Houston at the park the other morning. And if *that* were so, it put a whole new perspective on things. One for which Gracie wasn't sure she cared.

" . . . know if he's married?" Marge's voice said.

Gracie realized that her friend was still talking. With her mind in a whirl, she didn't really want to listen. "Sorry, Marge. Seem to be getting a bit of interference. I'd better go."

They confirmed the time to meet at Gracie's, said their good-byes, then Gracie hung up. She looked up to find herself approaching Main Street. A young man rounded the corner at a fast clip and almost bowled her over.

"Hey! Watch where you're going—oh, it's you, Mrs. Parks. Sorry."

Gracie was still catching her breath when she recognized Arnie Houston picking up his sunglasses off the sidewalk. "Hello. Really, Mr. Houston, you should be more careful. You seem to make a habit of knocking people over."

The young agent blushed right up into his blond hairline. "Said I was sorry."

Gracie began walking away.

He trotted quickly to catch up. "Hey, wait! Can I talk with you for a minute?"

"If you're game to walk, young man."

"Walk?"

"You know. For exercise."

He blinked then sneezed. "Excuse me. Uh, sure. I'm a gym rat, myself. Never actually *walk* outside." They strolled for a block. "Not much to see around here. Town's so small." He had to hustle to keep up. "Prefer my Stair-master. Nothing tones your glutes better. And you can read and exercise at the same time." Gracie waved to a trio of women on the other side of the street. "Tried to visit Anna Searfoss today. They wouldn't let me in. Can you believe that?"

Gracie faked an expression of astonishment.

"Talk about your bush-league hospital. Some nurse, right out of *One Flew Over the Cuckoo's Nest*, practically threw me out!" He ran his fingers through his spiky hair. "Man! I was just trying to talk to the lady."

"I told you that she wasn't well enough for visitors."

"But I'm not . . ." he hesitated. "Look, could we sit for a minute?" He led Gracie to a nearby bench, directly across from the clock honoring the town's war dead. "Need a drag."

As they were outdoors, Gracie didn't think she could refuse his request. While watching him light up, she couldn't understand how he could ruin his lungs yet still claim to be a gym rat.

Houston inhaled heavily then turned and blew a cloud of smoke toward a cheery tree, almost in bloom. Then, he sneezed again, excusing himself. "I know, I've got to quit."

Poor flowers! Gracie thought. *They'll probably curl up and die.* "What did you want to speak to me about?"

"Lived here long?"

"Most of my life."

Houston's jaw dropped. "You've got to be kidding."

Gracie shook her head.

"Man! In this dum . . . uh . . . place?" He exhaled another cloud of smoke. "Can't imagine. What'd you do for excitement?"

"Sure . . ." Gracie began.

"It's beyond me." He interrupted her before she could offer her version of Willow Bend's social whirl. "Look, Mrs.

Parks. You're Anna and Joe's friend, right? Well, I . . . I was hoping you'd convince them to sign with me. You heard all the stuff I can do for them. I'm sure *you* appreciate the benefits I'm offering." He paused, eyeing the burning ash. "Can't understand their hesitation. I mean, look at this place," he said, waving his arms. "Where are they going to get my kind of expertise in a hick town that doesn't even serve biscotti! It's, like, totally alien. Give me the Big Apple any day of the week. You seem on the ball, Mrs. Parks. Would you talk to them? I really want to sign them, especially before that nephew—"

A cell phone rang.

Gracie didn't even check hers. She knew better.

Houston was soon into a heated conversation. She waited for a couple of moments, then shook her head. Her question about Tom Williams would have to wait. Patting his arm in farewell, she rose and left the young producer, perched on the bench, shouting something about market shares.

Gracie shuddered. She paused and looked around. Several cars rolled along Main Street. A number of shoppers waved happily while others hurried in and out of the stores. The tall clock was right on time. She smiled at Lester's truck as it rolled past and received a cheerful honk in reply.

I'll take Willow Bend, thank you very much.

HER STOMACH WAS GROWLING. *That'll teach you, Gracie Parks*, she thought. *Eating junk for lunch.* Maybe too much sugar was causing her to harbor suspicious thoughts about Tom Williams.

Seeing she was just a block from Abe's Deli, she decided to stop in. What could be a better way to regain your perspective than delicious food and good conversation with an old friend?

"Hey, there, Gracie!" Abe waved at her from a table where he was taking an order. "Be right there."

She waved back and, after greeting a couple of people, plunked down on a free stool.

"Been walking long?" Abe asked upon his return.

Gracie looked at her watch. 3:10 P.M. "Guess so," she replied, slightly surprised at the time.

"Must be hungry than. Was just going to have what's left

of the potato and corn chowder and a cheese biscuit. Join me?"

"Sounds perfect," she said, realizing that she might not get time for dinner. "You'll never believe what Uncle Miltie and I had for lunch."

She told him as he ladled out the thick soup and brought over two steaming bowls. "Ice cream!" he replied, breaking off a bit of biscuit. "And you, Gracie Parks, a professional caterer!"

Gracie grinned and sipped the chowder. "Delicious! What do you have in here? Tarragon?"

Abe smiled. "Don't miss a trick, do you?"

They ate for a few moments. Then Abe mentioned he hadn't heard anything more about the fires. Gracie quickly filled him in on her most recent brush with the phantom arsonist. The deli owner whistled. "Pretty scary." As Abe tilted his bowl to get the last bits of corn, he added, "The town is sure jumpy, one way or another. Speaking of which, how are Joe and Anna doing? Sure are causing their own bit of excitement, what with the TV show and all that."

"Too much excitement," Gracie replied, swallowing the last bite of biscuit. She filled him in on Anna's collapse and current stay in the hospital.

Abe shook his head and began clearing the plates. "Didn't know. Give her my regards, would you?" He nodded toward the coffee pot.

"Love some," she replied. He took a check from a customer and rang it through the till. Then he handed her a full mug and began sipping his own. "I'm really worried about them, Abe," she continued, mug cupped in her hands. "Neither of them are young, and with this added stress, I'm afraid Anna's diabetes is going to cause trouble. You wouldn't believe how totally moonstruck everyone is about this television show! I don't even know if Anna will sign with the agent who suggested the idea in the first place, much less demand that the series be shot in Willow Bend."

Abe blew on his coffee for a moment. "It's too bad, you know. Lot of folks are counting on her. They all think the show's a great idea. Good for the economy, jobs, and bound to provide a higher tourism profile." He hesitated, flushing slightly.

Gracie eyed him. "What?"

Abe let out a sigh. "I have to admit, I'm sort of hoping my deli will be considered as a set." He grinned sheepishly. "That hotshot agent was in here. Had a potato kugel, then asked for bottled water, if you can believe it! But he liked the place. Said it was *dead real*."

Gracie blinked. "Huh?"

"Think it means 'good.' Hope so, anyway. He was with that nephew of Joe and Anna's."

Gracie's inner attenae sprang to attention. "Who? Tom Williams?"

"That's the one. Boy, can that fellow eat!" He shrugged and wiped the counter top. "They're a funny pair, those two."

"Can't imagine what they have in common." *But what I'd give to find out!*

"Couldn't tell you," Abe replied. "But something with plenty of history." He drained his mug. "Based on the heat of their conversation."

So, Gracie thought. *Tom Williams does know Arnie Houston!* The questions started to tumble forth. How well did they know each other? Why did Tom pretend not to know Houston at her house? And, why hasn't Tom said anything about this previously? Maybe Houston was going to tell her before he was interrupted by the cell phone call?

She didn't have the answers yet, but, for the sake of her friends, Gracie Parks was determined to find them.

J UST A LITTLE TO THE LEFT. A little more. There!"
Lester Twomley declared as Rick Harding and Don
Delano placed a table directly under a framed copy of "The
Star-Spangled Banner." Lester threw a crisp white cloth over
the wooden surface, fiddled with the folds for a moment,
then stood back to admire their handiwork.

A large knot of regulars at Willow Bend's seniors center
clapped politely from their front row seats. Lester made a little bow and the group laughed. It was 6:39 P.M. The room
buzzed with the sound of scraping chairs, muffled conversations and whirring wheelchairs. In one corner, Barb Jennings
sat, fingers ambling along the keys of an old piano, warming
up with a slow version of "As Time Goes By." One elderly
couple waltzed in leisurely fashion nearby, watched closely
by three young children.

Gracie looked up from arranging the cutlery and sticking decorative little toothpick flags into the centerpieces. She was astounded to see that the room was almost packed. She winked at Uncle Miltie, who was standing at the entrance, greeting guests and handing them name tags. Gracie thought her uncle looked dashing in his jacket and made a mental note to tell him so. Marge, dressed in a floral shirtwaist, was chatting to an elderly man in a khaki uniform while placing slices of apricot pie onto a small sea of plates. Occasionally, her eyes roamed the room. Most of the veterans were wearing their service jackets. One man had a tiny Canadian flag pinned to his shoulder, and another bravely wore his regimental kilt. His knobby, gnarled knees attracted more than one giggle, especially from the younger guests.

Gracie glanced down at her own silk blouse and linen trousers. They were perfect, even though for the moment partially covered by an apron. She fingered the pearls around her neck, a gift from Elmo, and worn today as a memento for all lost men. Nearby stood Mac Medline, alone. He looked fine, neatly shaven, clean bandage on his thumb, navy cap covering his whitish hair, but after the scene at the hospital, Gracie wondered. She noticed Joe Searfoss was sitting on the opposite side of the room with his nephew, Mayor Ritter and a gray-haired couple, his hands wildly gesticulating. Perhaps Joe wouldn't see Mac. Gracie wasn't sure she was going to be able to get through the night without confronting Tom Williams. But she knew that this was neither the place nor the time.

"Come on, Lester!" Don commanded, quickly wiping his glasses. "Stop admiring and start moving. We've got more tables to set up." The three men moved quickly and soon a row of tables dominated one wall. Pastor Paul stepped into the room, shook Uncle Miltie's hand, and moved slowly about, greeting the residents and guests.

The sudden sound of a tin whistle froze everyone in their tracks. The old soldiers snapped to attention and turned to face the mournful music. A lone veteran, dressed in an army jacket and cap, marched in, slowly playing "The Last Post." Everyone stood. The hair on the back of Gracie's neck leapt up. She looked around. All eyes were on the sole musician. Uncle Miltie and the other servicemen brought their right hands sharply to their brows as their comrade-in-arms proudly paraded past. The whistler stopped beneath "The Star-Spangled Banner" and finished the last few bars. Then, he tucked the tin whistle into a pocket and saluted smartly. A flash of movement rippled around the room as the rest of the veterans followed suit. The silence was absolute.

Then, an elderly woman began clapping. Like the unfurling of a flag, the applause rippled and snapped until it filled the entire space. Eyes moist, the veterans grinned and proudly embraced and shook each other's hands.

Gracie wiped tears from her eyes and gave her uncle, and then Joe, a crushing hug. Soon, everyone was wiping away tears and embracing the old soldiers. Finally, Pastor Paul gave a short prayer of thanks in which he reminded them of the precious value of each and every human life.

Grinning, the veterans moved in to the tables. Small groups of elderly men, some assisted by relatives, others by members of the Eternal Hope choir, began carefully arranging photographs, medals, newspaper clippings and keepsakes, like dogtags and cigarette lighters, on the tables. Some photographs and clippings were mounted and stood against the wall.

Her heart in her throat, Gracie watched several of the men hesitate, their eyes staring at a photograph, momentarily transported to another time. Others touched the dogtags as though they were talismen. Perhaps they were, Gracie realized. They had done so much for so many, these now frail and elderly gentlemen. She was privileged to be a small part of a celebration in their honor and thrilled that it was due to her own war hero, George Morgan.

"Where'd you want this?" Tish Ball asked, a large coffee urn in her hands.

"Or these?" said Tyne Anderson, holding a tray of cream and sugar.

Again, Gracie quickly wiped her eyes then checked the food tables. "Over there," she pointed to an empty space near the end. "Just beside the punch bowl. Oh, and Tish? Would you mind plugging it in?"

She stood back and eyed the arrangement with satisfaction. A trio of older women, one supported by walking sticks, began sampling the brownies.

"Think we're ready?" Marge asked, cleaning her hands on a colorful napkin.

Gracie smiled. "We'd better be."

"Did I tell you? Got a call from that aggressive young man, Arnie Houston."

"What'd he want?" Gracie asked, though she was certain she knew the answer.

"Wanted me to convince Anna and Joe to sign with him." Marge laughed. "Of all the nerve!"

"What'd you say?"

"Well, you know I like the idea of a television series, but . . . I told him if he didn't stop pushing Anna and Joe, I'd encourage them *not* to sign with him." She glanced toward Tom Williams. "Oh, and thanks for inviting Tom."

"Hey!" Don's voice echoed in Gracie's ear. "What about the help? And by the way, Gracie, any more news about the CD for Anna and Joe?"

"I haven't had a minute to think about it!" she replied. "Thanks for reminding me, though. I'll get going on it soon as this is over."

"I understand," Don said. "Maybe the group can talk about it later, brainstorm some song ideas."

Marge patted his arm and nodded to Rick and Lester. "You guys have done a super job." She pointed to the desserts spread in front of them. "Go for it." She turned to the rest of the room. "Everybody!" Marge said, raising her voice. "Please, help yourselves to food and drink."

It was as though she'd announced a cash giveaway. Within a minute, the food tables were under siege. Marge and Gracie scurried to the kitchen to provide replenishments. Startled, Estelle looked up from a kitchen chair, her face a picture of guilt, her mouth full of apricot pie.

"Okay, Estelle," Gracie said. "Can you chew and cut at the same time?"

After twenty minutes of continuous activity, the crowd at the tables dwindled to those seeking coffee refills. A group of attendees circled Barb, shouting out song suggestions, which the talented musician played immediately. Several individuals strolled by the display tables, carefully reading the news clippings and examining the keepsakes. Uncle Miltie and a couple of other veterans stood by their tables, their enthusiasm and pride evident in their military bearing and nonstop conversation. The choir members had settled into a group of chairs near the kitchen and had invited Tom Williams to join them. Marge and Gracie joined them for a few minutes before undertaking the clean-up.

"...benefit CD for your aunt and uncle," Don Delano was saying to Tom. "How about we kick around a few song ideas?"

"Great!" Rick said, sitting forward. "I've been thinking they should be old tunes, you know, from when Anna and Joe were young."

"That sounds good," Gracie said.

"Think that would sell?" Tish Ball asked.

"Depends on our market," Lester replied. "Some of the old stuff's coming back. I hear Tony Bennett's all the rage."

"Tony Bennett," Tyne Anderson asked. "Isn't he dead?"

Lester shook his head. "You kidding? That old crooner will definitely outlast most of us."

"It'd be nice to know what Anna and Joe liked," Tish said. "Maybe they had their own song. John and I love 'Stairway to Heaven.'

Don reached for a dessert platter. "I'll bet you the rest of these brownies that that's Tyne and Bill's song, too."

"No bet," Lester replied, winking.

Tyne smiled and nodded. "We had a double wedding."

"How about you and Rick?" Estelle Livett asked the young couple sitting side by side.

Comfort Harding smiled and reached for Rick's hand. "That's easy. 'You Don't Send Me Flowers Anymore.' We danced to it at our wedding." Her husband shifted uncomfortably.

"Can't beat Streisand and Diamond," Lester replied, with a grin. "Excellent choice!"

"Very romantic!" added the twins with a pleasurable sigh. Rick fiddled with his plate.

"What about you and Elmo, Gracie?" Don asked.

Gracie pursed her lips. " I'll never forget . . . we first heard it while driving to a sock hop." She smiled at the memory. 'Walkin' After Midnight.'

"Oh yeah," Rick said, his voice full of approval. "Patsy Cline. What a *voice!*" He began to serenade Gracie, imitating Patsy Cline's twang with affection, and soon the others joined in. By the time they reached a rousing crescendo, with Rick and Don singing faster and more frequently than the others, Barb had stopped playing and everyone was listening to them. The group laughed and accepted a round of applause.

"What songs do you think your uncle and aunt would like, Tom?" Estelle Livett asked, after the noise died down. "After all, they're *your* relatives."

The members of the choir watched Tom Williams. Gracie closely eyed the brown-haired man. *This will be interesting.*

"Uh," he stammered, complexion darkening. "I . . . I really don't know. All I can think of are some kids' songs Aunt Anna sang for me."

"Surely you must have some idea of what *they* liked?" Marge asked, biting into a brownie. "You visited them? Heard some of their songs?"

He shifted nervously and shook his head. Gracie found his reaction very intriguing. But, come on, she said to herself, do you recall the favorite songs of all your own older relatives?

Lester urged him, "You must remember some tunes. Anna's what? in her mid-seventies?" A couple of heads nodded. "Well, that puts us into the forties, *maybe* fifties, right?" The heads nodded again.

"More likely forties," Don said. "They'd have been listening to music when they were younger."

"Okay," Lester continued. "So, what're we talking?"

"Big band for sure, you know Glenn Miller, 'Pennsylvania 6-5000,' or maybe Benny Goodman?" Rick suggested. "Perhaps even a little jazz?"

"How about Judy Garland?" Marge offered. "My mom's older than Anna but she must have taken me to see *The Wizard of Oz* half a dozen times. She loves that kind of Broadway tune, you know, 'Over the Rainbow,' 'For Me and My Gal,' 'Zing! Went the Strings of My Heart.'" She paused, glancing around. "Hey! Bet you no one knows Judy Garland's real name?"

The twins shook their heads. Rick and his wife looked blank. Don shrugged.

"Judy Garland?" Lester suggested.

The others groaned.

"No, silly," Marge replied. "Frances Ethel Gumm."

"My parents were always partial to the Gershwin

brothers," Gracie said. "My dad used to play 'I've Got a Crush on You' and 'They Can't Take That Away from Me' all the time. He used to sing them to my mom." She smiled at the memories.

Estelle shook her head. "Enough reminiscing! We could go round and round all day. It sure would make it easier if Tom had some ideas. How are we going to find out without spilling the beans?"

"Barb might know," Gracie suggested. "She knows a lot of music history."

"Hey!" Lester exclaimed. "Anna and Joe are staying at your house, right?" Gracie nodded. "You can play a few old tunes, Gracie. See if they mention any in particular."

Gracie nodded again. "Not sure what records we have, but I'll give it a try." She stretched. "Sorry, folks. Got to get back to work." She glanced at Marge. They rose and, for the next fifteen minutes, concentrated on making sure all the revelers had been offered the desserts and coffee or tea. Then they started tidying up the tables.

While she was doing some final clean-up touches, Gracie overhead bits and pieces of her friends' conversations. They had changed topics.

". . . don't know about filming the show in town," Don Delano said, savoring a fresh mug of coffee.

Rick Harding nodded while offering his wife a cup of tea.

"Interesting dilemma," he began. "Comfort and I used to live on the east coast. Quite a few towns there depend on tourism as their sole economy, a couple have even had film crews down. You know, for movies." He shrugged.

"Sure we can't help you, ladies?" Lester asked.

Gracie shook her head with a smile, picked up the last plates and headed into the kitchen.

". . . of publicity," Rick was saying upon her return. "After a year or two, it seemed to die down." Gracie collected flatware. "But then you have Prince Edward Island." *Oh no,* Gracie thought. *Not here. Not now.* She froze, and looked around quickly for Mac Medline. She spotted the farmer sitting beside Barb on the piano stool, belting out a marching song.

"That's in Canada, huh?" Lester asked, handing a bunch of spoons to Gracie.

Rick nodded. "Some friends of ours moved there. Real pretty countryside."

"What's it got to do with Anna's television show?" Marge asked, looking up from stacking plates.

"*Anne of Green Gables,*" Tish and Tyne said simultaneously.

Rick grinned at the others' confused faces.

"It's a children's story," Tish began.

"Written many years ago by L.M. Montgomery," her sister finished.

"So?" Lester asked, now grabbing paper napkins, crushing and tossing them, basketball fashion, into the garbage can. Most missed so that he had to retrieve them.

Rick leaned forward. "Sort of the same situation as Anna's. Montgomery's books were made into a television series. Soon, everyone wanted to see where the little red-headed girl lived. The islanders saw a good thing coming and jumped on it. They're making a fortune from that girl."

"What's wrong with that?" Marge asked. "We could all use a little good luck."

There was a murmur of agreement.

"Maybe," Comfort Harding said quietly. "My friends say it's caused some difficulties, divided the island. A lot of folks don't want to be known just as the setting for a children's book, no matter how nice it is."

"Got a point," Don said.

An uncomfortable silence settled over the group.

Uh oh, Gracie thought.

"Have they signed the deal yet?" Lester asked Gracie. "Heard something about a deadline."

Gracie shook her head. "They've asked for more time."

"Hey!" Barb's voice shouted across the room. "We could use a few more voices over here."

The members of the group exchanged glances. Then Rick rose, held out his hand to his wife and said, "Come on, baby. Let's show 'em what we got."

The twins giggled and got up.

"You coming, Gracie? Marge?" Lester asked as the others joined the swaying gang around the piano.

The women pleaded exhaustion and flopped down onto a nearby old couch, content to let the music flow over them as they regained their energies. Barb plunked the first few notes to 'I'll Be Seeing You,' and the entire group immediately began singing.

"You ladies look as though you've been through the war," a man's voice shouted.

Gracie looked up and smiled.

"Hello, Rocky! Glad you could make it."

"See you found the leftovers," Marge said, eyeing the overflowing plate in the editor's hand.

Rocky bit into a brownie and chewed for a moment. "Nothing to it. Basic journalistic know-how."

Marge grinned. Then, she stood, stretching dramatically. "Think I'll get a glass of water. Anyone?"

The other two shook their heads. Rocky slid down beside Gracie and offered her his plate. "Brownie?" he shouted, leaning closer. "Piece of pie? I brought extra. Figured you hadn't had time to sample."

A man after my own heart, she thought. "Thank you," she said instead, taking a small square. Once the chocolate hit her tongue, she immediately felt energized. She quickly devoured another one.

"Get you coffee? Tea?"

"No, thanks."

"Haven't heard from my pal about Houston yet," Rocky said. "Expect something tomorrow. Heard anything more about the fires?"

Gracie shook her head. "How about you?"

"I've got Mike nosing around the police station but, so far, mum's the word." He shrugged, broke off a piece of milk cake and popped it into his mouth. "Um. These desserts are great!" He snagged another chunk of the milk cake and held it out. "What is this, anyway?"

Before she could answer, Barb began playing the "Boogie Woogie Bugle Boy of Company B." The chorus of voices swelled with the rocking tune. Rick and Comfort joined an older couple, who had started to jitterbug. Tish grabbed a protesting Lester, and Tyne snagged Joe Searfoss. Several men shoved the chairs nearer to the wall, creating a large dance area that was immediately filled. Uncle Miltie, and a few others, rocked their walkers back and forth in time with the beat.

Gracie grinned. What a wonderful sight! For a moment, there was no talk of television shows or fires. No dissension or turmoil. Folks of all ages from Willow Bend mixing, laughing, loving. Now, *this* was more like her town.

"May I have the pleasure?"

Gracie blinked, then looked up to find Rocky Gravino standing over her, his right hand extended.

"I'd be delighted," she replied, any lingering weariness vanquished in an instant.

31

THE FAIRY TALE BALL couldn't last forever. Within fifteen minutes, many dancers had tired and left the floor to congregate and chat in a semi-circle of chairs. Mac Medline stood up, strode to the middle, an orator finding his stage.

"It'll be the ruin of the town, I'm warning you," he began. His voice grew louder. "We'll lose all respect, believe you me. All our other industries, farms, pretty nearly everything'll eventually have to pack up and leave."

The remaining dancers stopped, exchanging embarrassed glances. Even Mayor Ritter stopped talking. Rocky's hands dropped from Gracie's as he turned toward the disturbance. Confused, Barb Jennings stopped playing, fingers hanging in the air above the ivory and ebony keys.

"Keep playing!" someone shouted. A couple revived their waltz.

"What are you talking about?" another queried.

Barb's fingers dropped and the piano thundered again.

"Just say no to Lazy Lake," Mac's voice boomed. "Tell Anna and Joe we don't want them and their book and their TV actors to make a mockery of our community."

Joe Searfoss rose from his chair, his face a ghastly white. Still seated, his nephew stirred nervously beside him.

Gracie could feel the tension building in the room and racked her brain to find any chance of quickly diffusing the situation. If only Barb kept playing! "That's it, Barb," she cried. "Another jive." She grabbed Rocky's hand. He turned, and reading her eyes, began twirling her. Another pair began jiving.

"Just say no!" the large farmer bellowed.

Oh, no! Gracie thought. *Keep playing! You've got to keep playing.*

But Barb pushed herself away from the piano. Rocky and Gracie hesitated, then stopped. The last musical notes lingered for a moment.

"No need to shout, Mac," Rocky's voice cut across the room. "Now, I don't know what you're on about, but this isn't the right time."

Gracie knew it was now too late. She moved in Joe's direction just as Rocky made a beeline for Mac. Tom Williams rose to his feet.

Medline whirled toward Rocky. "Sure as shootin' is." He

pointed to Joe Searfoss. "We've got Joe right here. Now's the time to tell him. To make sure he knows that Willow Bend's dead set against being turned into a theme park. Before it's too late."

There was a murmur of agreement.

"Who voted you mayor?" a man's voice angrily demanded.

Several voices shouted, "Yeah. Who?"

"Someone mention me?" the mayor asked.

Another voice rose above the mumbling. "This is none of our business," Paul Meyer said, striding across to Joe's side. He embraced the shaken man on the shoulder. "I'm surprised and disappointed in you, Mac." Mac flushed. "We're all here to celebrate the great sacrifice and contribution given decades ago by the brave men of Willow Bend. We're not here, nor have we the right, to judge our dear friends, Joe and Anna Searfoss."

"Amen!" Uncle Miltie sang out.

"But what about the television show?" an elderly female resident asked. "We should be tickled pink and grateful to Anna and Joe for putting our town on the map! I, for one, can't wait until those Hollywood folks arrive. There hasn't been this much excitement here since . . ." she hesitated. "Well," she finally said, her cheeks flaming red. "I don't rightly know when."

"You don't understand!" Mac replied. "I've seen it before.

It's like a cancer, gets into everyone. Mark my words. Don't be greedy, Joe."

"That's enough, Mac," Rocky said, his voice low but strong.

"What've you got to say about that, Joe? Huh?" Mac asked, ignoring the editor.

"Leave my uncle alone," Tom snapped.

Rick and Don moved to Rocky's side.

"Come on, Mac," Rocky said. "Time to go." He grabbed one of the farmer's arms while Rick did the same thing. They gently but firmly moved Mac toward the door which Don opened swiftly. "You've said enough for one night."

"Don't sign it, Joe!" Mac shouted. "Or you'll regret it!"

"Come on, Joe," Pastor Paul whispered. "Why don't you sit down for a moment? Have a cup of coffee."

As though in a faint, Joe Searfoss dropped into a chair but when Tom handed him a cup of coffee, he tasted it gratefully. When he nibbled a piece of milk cake, a bit of color returned to his weathered cheeks.

Barb now played some soft music and slowly, a variety of new conversations started. In small groups, people began saying their good-byes and leaving.

Rocky, Don and Rick returned. Rick's wife hurried to her husband. He led her away, speaking quietly.

"Shame to have this ruin the vets' big night," Don said. "But I guess we shouldn't be surprised, what with all emotions running so high. You going to write about it?" he asked Rocky.

Gracie watched her husky friend. She often thought that, as the editor and owner of the local paper, Rocky Gravino had the most influential job in Willow Bend. She rarely had cause to call him for abusing his position. She watched to see what he would say.

Rocky paused then shook his head. "I'm here as a guest and admirer."

Don smiled. "At least that's something." He then excused himself and headed over to help Lester rearrange the furniture.

"Well, Gracie," Rocky said, "may I give you a hand before calling it a night?"

"Thank you," she replied. "That would be a great—"

"This stuff go in the van?" Estelle asked, interrupting, her arms loaded with cake tins and pans.

"Hang on a sec," Marge replied, walking toward them carrying several platters. "I'll come with you."

"Anyone know where the dish soap is?" Tyne's voice rang out from the kitchen.

Gracie glanced around as her friends cheerfully tackled the clean up. Despite their differences, they continued to respect, care for and help one another. She looked over at Joe Searfoss. He was listening quietly to Pastor Paul while his nephew chatted to Uncle Miltie. There would be time enough to investigate further the secrets surrounding Tom Williams.

Time enough to support Joe and Anna in making their decision.

But at this moment, Gracie Parks just wanted to enjoy the honest and true spirit of camaraderie displayed by her fellow citizens of Willow Bend.

"Here, Tish!" she called to her friend, who was struggling to balance too many used cups and saucers. "Rocky and I will help you."

G RACIE ATTEMPTED to let the buzz of the lawn mower occupy her mind. Wednesday had dawned with a crystal clear sky. Even if Gooseberry hadn't chewed on the grass upon their return from praise-walking, she already knew the cutting was overdue. So, after a quick breakfast and tidy-up, Gracie dressed in one of Elmo's old T-shirts and a baggy pair of sweat pants and marched quickly behind the power mower, trying not to think.

Didn't matter, her thoughts kept pushing through, especially her worries about Anna. Both Anna's doctor and her lawyer, Ann O'Neill, had advised the Searfosses to delay their decision until Anna's health stabilized, so Joe had told Arnie Houston that they needed more time. The young agent had been furious and threatened to take the deal off the table, as he put it. Ashen, Joe had hung up the phone, terrified to tell his wife. So far, he hadn't, but he was now on his way to the hospital.

She wheeled and began charging back across her lawn, chasing thoughts about the previous evening. It should have been a success. And would have been without Mac Medline. Gracie wished the lingering negative sentiments raised at the center would disappear but she feared she knew better. She couldn't help feeling sorry for Mac, though. The poor man was obviously lonely, and upset, but she didn't think he had any close family to turn to. He wasn't a churchgoer, that much she knew, so there wasn't any question of her asking Paul Meyer or any of the other town's pastors to go and pay him a social call. Mac would probably run over the visiting clergy with his tractor!

Uncle Miltie gestured from the sidewalk where he was slowly trimming a hedge.

She stopped mowing and cut the power.

"You're going to give yourself sore shoulders, my dear," he shouted over the fading noise, "if you keep racing around like that. Doesn't cut any better if you go any faster. Probably the opposite."

She exhaled heavily, then wiped her forehead with her shirt tail. Her shoulders were aching just a little.

"I know last night ended ugly, but you can't outrun your worries," her uncle continued, "even if you try and mow them down." He paused to see if she caught his little joke. Gracie forced a smile. "Come on, Gracie. You've been miles away, all morning. Don't let an old grouch like Mac Medline ruin what was otherwise a smashing success."

She sighed and leaned on the mower's handle.

"Maybe we can do something about it."

Gracie looked up, interested. "Like what?"

"Well, if I know you, you're not only disappointed in Mac's outburst, you're also a bit worried about him. Am I right?"

"You know me too well, Uncle M."

"Thought so. Got to admit, I've been wondering about him. He hasn't been to play pinochle in quite a while, but I just thought things were busy at the farm." He brushed a twig off his shirt. "I think we both could use some country air. How about you and I take a break and go out to Mac's farm and look in on him?"

"I think that's a wonderful idea! Give me a few minutes to freshen up. I've got just the peace offering to bring."

Within fifteen minutes, Fannie Mae was being guided out of Willow Bend and into a rolling landscape dotted by snoozing livestock and criss-crossed by old rail fencing. On Uncle Miltie's lap rested a basket holding two fresh loaves of brown bread and two jars of homemade pickles.

Gracie rolled her window further down and inhaled the sweet, thick scent of manure and recently tilled soil.

"Out here," Uncle Miltie declared, "the land's fertile, the water's clean and the work's hard but honest."

Gracie let her eyes wander across the pastoral panorama spreading out in front of Fannie Mae. "No one can look at a calf romping in a meadow or at a ten-foot row of fall corn and doubt the existence of the hand of God."

"Amen," Uncle Miltie responded. "Sure is divine." He paused for a couple of tire beats. "Did you and Elmo ever think about moving to the country?"

Gracie smiled and nodded at her uncle. "We talked a lot about owning a small farm. Nothing much, a few chickens for eggs, maybe a cow or two for fresh milk." She sighed softly. "Something we'd planned for our retirement."

He patted her shoulder. "At least you were able to dream about it."

"That's true. And dream we did." She directed the Caddy around a narrow curve. "I've never been to Mac's farm. Would have trouble finding it without you."

"Only been once, but it's not so hard," he responded, directing her to another winding left turn. "Just that some of these back roads are poorly marked."

"Tell me about Mac. I don't know much other than his wife died a few years ago."

Miltie nodded. "He's a hard man to know. Doesn't invite visitors. None too friendly at the best of times. Bitter most of the time. It took me ages to get him to play pinochle. At first,

I thought he might be shy. Then, maybe, that he didn't like games. Ends up neither's the case. He's just plain ornery, feels he's been hard done by."

"In what way?" Gracie asked. "Other farmers have had bad luck."

"True enough. If you ask me, he expects the world to come to him, *not* the other way 'round. He's not a careful man, nor much of a thinker. His wife had a better head for business. As you saw, lets his emotions run high, sometimes they take the better of him." He hesitated. "I think he's an instinctive farmer, gives crops a try more on hunch than from much thought or research. Mind you, he's had some boom years."

"What about his family?"

"He and his wife, Mabel, they were never blessed with children. Couldn't, some say. Mac wouldn't hear of adoption, at least, that's the gossip at the seniors center. I think it caused problems in their marriage. Certainly made it more expensive to farm, having to pay for all the hands. You forget how much farm kids do."

"What does he farm?"

"Hay, mostly, now. He's still got a few head of beef cattle. Don't think he ever had milkers." His blue eyes twinkled. "Now, that's where the kids come in handy! Up before dawn, milking the cows before school. Then, again, after dinner. Saves the farmer a lot of time."

A long, rutted drive, bounded by rotting fences and rusted barbed wire, appeared before them.

"Here we are," Uncle Miltie said.

As Gracie navigated the automobile around the larger pot-holes, she eyed the farmhouse and outbuildings. All had seen better days. She reached for the horn but was stopped by her uncle's hand.

"No need, dear. I see he's got his own early warning—"

The deep guttural snarls assaulted their ears only seconds before three sleek black bodies raced around the slouching barn and launched themselves against Gracie's car doors. Rows of yellow teeth flashed as spittle slapped and toenails scratched onto the glass.

"Oh my goodness!" Gracie shrieked, leaning toward the middle. She bumped shoulders with her uncle, who was doing the same.

"Hang on, dear!" he shouted over the howling. "Mac'll be here any minute."

True to his word, a man's voice suddenly bellowed. The dogs dropped to the dusty track and sat, their haunches still shivering. Mac Medline, dressed in dirty and ripped overalls, strode slowly from inside the barn. By the time he reached Gracie's car, she was certain the slavering dogs couldn't con-tain themselves any longer. But with a snap of his thick fin-gers, Mac Medline sent the big hounds scurrying back to the sagging porch that fronted a peeling two-story farmhouse.

"Hello, Gracie. Miltie," Mac said, looking not in the least bit surprised. He pushed back his engineer's hat, revealing a dirty brow. "What can I do for you?"

Gracie hesitated. Uncle Miltie took over, cautiously opening his door. "Hi, Mac! Gracie and I thought we'd drop by. See how you're doing." He climbed out of the car. "How's the thumb?"

Gracie opened her door. Mac reluctantly stood back and she stepped out.

"Fine."

The bandage covering the damaged digit was soiled and loose. He held it protectively against his massive chest.

"Must be awkward to change that bandage yourself," Gracie said.

"I get by."

"Well, er," her uncle hesitated. "Is there anything we can do to help?" He turned and opened the back door. "Gracie's brought you some fresh bread and pickles," he said, pulling the items from the back seat. Mac sauntered over and took them.

"Mighty nice of you, Gracie. But there's no need. I get along just fine on my own."

"I'm sure you do, Mac, but we hoped they'd be welcome."

The farmer eyed his gifts. "They are, thank you."

There was an awkward silence as the three stood in a triangle in the middle of Mac Medline's jumbled inner farm-yard. A pair of chickens scooted past, followed by a gray and white cat, stealthily creeping behind. The chickens squawked, then flitted onto the seat of a rusting old tractor. It was obvi-ous that Mac was not going to invite them in. From the looks of his property, Gracie wasn't overly disappointed. She wasn't sure if she'd trust the house not to fall in the minute they entered through the damaged front doorway.

"That's a fine cat," she said, trying to find something to begin the conversation.

"Got plenty more. All the same to me." Mac's eyes nar-rowed. "You here to tell me something?"

"No," Uncle Miltie replied. "Social visit, just as I said."

"Anna and Joe sign that contract?"

Gracie shook her head. "We came by to see you, Mac. As a neighborly gesture, that's all. We knew you hurt your thumb and were . . . *disappointed* the other night. As my uncle said, we just wanted to know if you needed help."

He smiled coldly. Gracie caught a glimpse of broken teeth. "Mighty kind of you, I'm sure. But I don't need your charity, just like I don't need any TV show wrecking my town." His voice grew louder. "You come here, bringing food, and expect me to listen while you try and convince me that Anna and Joe have every right to sign that darned piece of paper. Well, maybe they do, maybe they don't. Don't matter to me none." He jabbed his fist into his chest then winced. "I've got my own rights. I told you. I'll say and do whatever I have to do to stop them outside folks from taking over Willow Bend."

"No one says they're coming, Mac," Gracie replied, keeping her voice level. A cow lowed in a nearby field. "You're jumping to conclusions. Anna and Joe haven't signed the contract yet. They may never."

"She's right, Mac," Uncle Miltie added. "You're getting all riled up for nothing. Why don't you come down to the center one of these days, play some more pinochle. The guys miss you."

Mac's eyes narrowed, as though he thought Uncle Miltie was pulling his leg. After a moment, he realized the older man's question was sincere. He shrugged. "Can't afford the time. This," he held up his bandaged thumb, "set me back quite a piece. Tractor's down. Hard enough doing everything on my ow—" He stopped, realizing what he had said.

"Perhaps we *can* help," Gracie interrupted, seizing her opportunity. An idea was forming. "You need help fixing your tractor, right? Maybe with a few odd jobs, like painting?"

Mac eyed her suspiciously but eventually nodded.

"I'm sure there are a number of men at the seniors center who'd love a chance to get their hands dirty, don't you think, Uncle Miltie?" He nodded, a smile entering his blue eyes.

"Maybe some of them could come and give you a hand."

"Don't want no charity."

"Who said anything about charity? You'll be helping them, don't you see?"

"She's right, Mac. Why, some of those guys would give their eyeteeth to be out here in the country, fiddling with a carburetor or slapping on some whitewash. Be good for everyone, all around."

Mac was silent for a full minute, during which a rooster crowed three times. "I'm not changing my mind about that Lazy Lake business."

"We're not trying to make you change your mind about anything," Gracie replied. She wiped her hands on her jeans. "Well, we shouldn't keep you. Good-bye, Mac. Thanks for your hospitality."

Uncle Miltie touched the man's shoulder and, along with his walker, clambered into the car.

The farmer stood still as Gracie turned around, narrowly missing a combine's broken teeth, and slowly drove down the lane.

They drove in silence for ten minutes. Finally, she asked, "Do you think he'll take us up on the offer?"

"Don't know, honey," Uncle Miltie replied, "but you did good! I'm going to tell all the guys at the center. I think the canine early warning mob will be busy in the near future."

Gracie started to laugh. "I thought I was going to have a heart attack when they hit the car!"

"Age before beauty," her uncle replied, chuckling.

THEY HAD BARELY ROLLED UP Gracie's driveway when Uncle Miltie let out a gasp.

Gracie followed her uncle's eyes. Tish Ball, Tyne Anderson and Marge Lawrence strolled across her partially mowed lawn. Gracie's jaw dropped. The three women were clothed in costumes from the turn of the century.

"What in the *world*?" she asked, getting out of the car.

Marge grinned and twirled her ankle-length skirt to reveal pale yellow petticoats. Dressed in pink and white, Tish and Tyne curtseyed in perfect unison, their sunbonnets slipping over their faces.

"Well?" Marge asked. "They're not *exactly* right but what'd you think?"

The twins fumbled with the bonnets. Uncle Miltie chuckled and pulled his walker from the car.

"Lester!" Marge shouted.

Gracie and her uncle exchanged grins.

"Come on!" Marge encouraged. "They've got to see the whole picture."

In a moment, her front door opened and Lester Twomley shyly stepped onto the porch. He was wearing a flannel shirt, suspenders, twill trousers and work boots. Uncle Miltie burst out laughing. Gracie couldn't contain herself and joined in.

"Imagine!" Marge exclaimed. "The whole town dressed like this." The twins twirled delightedly. "Wouldn't it be fun?"

Gracie gasped then found her breath. "Is this a Lazy Lake scheme?"

"That's right!" Lester replied, stomping up her walk. "After the trouble last night, we thought we'd come by and show Anna and Joe just how great it could be."

Uncle Miltie leaned heavily on his walker, his shoulders still rocking with laughter.

"Well, you sure look the part," Gracie said dubiously. "But you're wasting your time. Anna's still in the hospital and Joe's visiting her. But Uncle Miltie and I will tell them all about it. Won't we?"

Her uncle nodded vehemently.

The quartet in costume looked crestfallen. Sweat was running down Lester's face. He pulled at his collar. "That's too bad," Marge declared. "I was really looking forward to seeing Anna's face. Thought this was just the ticket to perk her up. If she could just imagine how lovely the town will look, how much fun everyone will have, maybe it would make things easier for her."

"Another time, perhaps," Gracie replied.

Lester squirmed uncomfortably. "Don't know how those folks stood it," he whined. "This wool's killing me!"

Tish removed her bonnet and fluffed up her flattened blonde hair.

"Awfully hot," Tyne said.

Without another word, they turned and marched into Marge's house.

Marge curtseyed again, then followed her friends.

Before Gracie could say a word, her cell phone rang. She trotted up the porch steps, her uncle's laughter in her ears, and pawed through her purse.

"Hello?"

"Mrs. Parks? It's Tom, Anna and Joe's nephew."

"Yes, hello, Tom." Gracie slouched onto the porch steps.

"I'm sorry to bother you, ma'am, but I was wondering if I could ask you a favor."

Gracie grimaced. "Yes?"

There was a long pause. "I'm real worried about my aunt. She's under a lot of stress and I don't want to cause her any more."

"That's thoughtful of you."

Another hesitation. "Uh, thank you. It's . . . well, I've

already spoken to her, but I'm not sure she really listened."

"I'm sorry, Tom. I'm afraid I don't follow."

His words now poured out in a rush. "I've told her not to sign with that little snake, Arnie Houston! He's trouble, plain and simple. Dishonest. Got a real bad reputation, but my aunt . . . she's convinced that the town needs her to sign that contract. To demand that the show be shot here. It's all crazy, anyway! She doesn't have the clout to make that sort of demand." He breathed for a moment. "I know my aunt's only thinking of what's good for others but, really, Mrs. Parks, it would be better for her and Uncle Joe if they signed with . . . "

"Yes?"

"Look. Couldn't you just talk to them? They'll listen to you."

"I'm sorry, Tom, but I don't like being put in the middle. If your aunt and uncle want my advice, they'll ask for it. And I'll happily tell them what I think. Not what you or Mr. Houston, or anyone else for that matter, thinks."

Slowly moving up the walk, her uncle's head shot up at her tone.

"Houston? You been talking to him?"

"Tom, I don't know what's going on between you two, but the best thing you can do is tell them the truth."

Another long pause. "What?"

Gracie was becoming more impatient. "Come on, Thomas

Williams! There's something you're not saying. You *know* Arnie Houston, don't you?"

"Uh, sorry, Mrs. Parks. I've got to go. Thanks for your help."

Gracie was shaking her head, staring at the phone when it rang again.

"You were right," the editor and owner of the *Mason County Gazette* said. "He's real bad news."

"I'm sorry, Rocky," she replied, rising to her feet. "Who?"

"Arnie Houston. Got the skinny, as my press room buddies would say. The kid's a corker. His clients have a list of complaints as long as my arm."

Gracie plopped onto the porch swing. "You don't say."

"Yup. Let me see. . . ."

She heard the sounds of paper rustling. Blue eyes wide with questions, Uncle Miltie clumped over and settled in beside her.

"Here we are: unacceptable accounting practices, pretending to have production deals already in hand in order to encourage the client to sign, demanding a higher percentage fee than industry standards . . . the list goes on. Even an outstanding lawsuit or two. But my contacts tell me that Houston's not all flash. Does have a keen eye for what sells, it seems. And a reputation for spotting potential clients, then smooth-talking them into quickly signing a contract that gives him the exclusive rights to their product for a mere song." He paused. "I have to admit, though, he knows how to close a deal, both domestic and foreign. But, of course, his share's greater than that of his client."

"Whew!" was all Gracie could muster. *Thank You, Lord, for the sound advice of Your professionals.*

"Uh, Gracie," Rocky's voice deepened. "They haven't signed yet, have they?"

"No, praise God. They were advised to wait."

Rocky's deep laugh filled her ear. "That must have set the young pup howling!"

Gracie chuckled, then laughed out loud as a wave of relief swept over her. Uncle Miltie gave her a quizzical look. She flipped a thumbs-up sign. He grinned and began rocking the swing.

"Uh, awfully sorry about last night, Gracie," Rocky was saying. "The vets worked so hard and you all did such a fine job catering. Shame it was spoiled."

"Sure was." Her eyes were drawn down into her garden. Her cat was vigorously pawing at some newly planted geraniums.

"Shoo!"

"Pardon?"

"Oh, sorry, Rocky. I didn't mean you."

"Well, you're busy so I'll let you go."

Gracie stood and skipped down the steps, waving violently at Gooseberry. Her purse banged against her shoulder.

The big tom arched his back and hissed dramatically. Something clicked in Gracie's mind and she barely registered Rocky's last words.

"Oh, one other thing," he was saying. "Did you know that Tom Williams represents writers? Apparently runs one of the biggest literary agencies in the business."

She froze, cell phone in her hand. Gooseberry paused, then sidled up and around her legs.

"Gracie?" Uncle Miltie called after her.

There was something about Gooseberry. Something very important. He had reacted in a similar way just recently. If she could just grab onto that idea . . . Absent-mindedly, she ran her fingers over the cat's back then along his tail. When her fingers reached the scorched tip, it struck her. Then Herb Bower's words flashed into her brain: "*. . . usually done by kids. Bored, looking for thrills and attention.*"

"Oh, my goodness!" Gracie ignored her uncle's concerned words, grabbed her cell phone again, and punched in a number. "Hello? Phyllis?" She took a deep breath and slowed her speech. "This's Gracie. How are you and the baby?

"We'll be fine, thank you. Once I can get him to sleep." Phyllis replied, her voice rising over the sound of a baby crying. "You and Uncle Miltie?"

"Just wonderful, thanks. Is Katie with you?"

"No, she's out on her bike. Is it about the Lazy Lake role?"

"Not exactly." Gracie blinked. "Uh, well, yes!" she lied, crossing her fingers. She didn't ask for forgiveness. There wasn't time. "I was hoping to talk to her. Do you know where she might have gone?"

"Just a moment," Phyllis replied.

Gracie heard gurgling and then the sound of a burp.

"Well, she could be anywhere," Phyllis's voice returned in her ear. "But she was asking about Mr. Houston. Wanted to know where he was staying. I didn't really encourage her, but . . . I couldn't see the harm of her just biking by."

"Thank you, Phyllis," Gracie replied, hanging up.

"What's going on?" Uncle Miltie shouted from the porch.

She dialed another number. It was busy. *Oh, no!* "No time, Uncle Miltie!" she cried, digging her keys out of her purse while dashing to her car. Throwing the purse on the passenger's seat, she climbed in. "Sorry! Got to run!"

KATIE'S RED BIKE sprawled on the front lawn of Cordelia Fountain's tourist home. The door stood open. Gracie sprinted up the steps and burst inside, shouting the girl's name at the top of her lungs. No one answered. She raced into front room only to find it empty. She turned and crossed the hall into the study.

Katie stood in the middle, staring at a lump on the Turkish rug.

"Katie?" Gracie asked, blinking in disbelief.

It was Tom Williams' body that lay on the carpet, curled in a fetal position.

"I didn't touch him!" the girl shrieked, backing away. "Honest, I didn't! I didn't! He turned all white and fell. It wasn't me!"

Gracie was kneeling beside Tom in an instant, fingers checking his pulse. Thready and fast. His face was ashen, his hair damp. She noticed the smell of smoke and glanced up.

"I . . . I wouldn't have burned him. Honest!" Katie cried. She threw a half-used book of matches to the floor. "I was just playing." The girl burst into tears.

Gracie grabbed her cell phone from her purse and dialed 911. After giving the emergency dispatcher her address, she cradled Tom's head and whispered soothingly to him. "He turned white?"

Katie hid her head in her hands.

"It's all right, Katie. He's going to be fine. Now, be a good girl and tell me everything. You said he turned white and fell?"

The girl hiccuped while nodding. "Said he felt weird, dizzy or something."

In a blink, a rush of scenes flashed through Gracie's mind: Tom gulping water when he first arrived; his large appetite despite his thin body; his near fainting spell in her kitchen. It all came together. Just like the list of symptoms from the brochure at the hospital.

Tom groaned.

"Katie, dear. Hand me my purse."

The girl meekly followed orders.

Gracie dug out a juice box as Tom's eyes fluttered open. She fumbled with the straw. Katie snatched it from her hand, stripped off the cellophane covering, then jabbed it into the appropriate hole.

"Where am I?" he mumbled.

Gracie lifted his head. "Here," she whispered, taking the box from Kate. "Drink this. You're going to be fine."

It was like a miracle. Within minutes of drinking the juice, the color rose in Tom's cheeks. By the time the paramedics arrived, he was able to sit up.

"I think he's a diabetic," Gracie told the emergency technician. "I gave him some orange juice."

"Right!" the young woman replied. "Looks like it did the trick. We'll take care of him now. Want to come along?"

Gracie glanced at Tom.

"Please," he whispered. "You saved my life."

She shook her head. "Anna did. Without her, I wouldn't have had the juice nor the knowledge to offer it. Just give me a moment," she replied. Dialing the Nickolsons one more time, Gracie quickly asked Phyllis if she could come and get Katie. She assured the puzzled mother that she would explain everything later, then hung up.

Cordelia Fountain walked in. "What's going on?" she cried.

"Oh, Cordelia! I'm so glad you're home," Gracie said. "Could you wait with Katie until her mom comes? I'll explain everything later, okay?"

Gracie followed the gurney to the ambulance, with Cordelia's confused voice chasing her. "I'll take my car, Tom.

Meet you there. Don't worry, you're going to be fine."

As the paramedics were settling Tom in, he motioned to her. "Why'd you think I'm a diabetic?"

She told him about his symptoms and how she'd suddenly realized their significance. "Quick thinking," the attendant said as she adjusted the gurney straps.

"Diabetes." Tom tried to shake his head. "I'd never have thought of it. Figured I was having a breakdown."

She nodded, an idea popping into her mind. "Not so far-fetched, you know."

His eyes narrowed.

"Runs in the family."

"Oh," he smiled wanly. He paused for a moment. "Now, do you believe who I am?"

It was Gracie's turn to smile. She patted his shoulder. "You've still got a lot of explaining to do. Your aunt and uncle deserve the truth. The whole truth."

He closed his eyes. "Yes," he whispered. The attendants took his pulse, then stroked his hand encouragingly. Gracie stepped back. The ambulance doors closed and the boxy vehicle began to move.

"Gracie Parks, what *is* going on?" Cordelia asked, coming up to her. "The man's a guest in my home, I deserve to know. And," she held up the match book. "What're these doing on the carpet in my study?"

"Oh, Cordelia," Gracie started. "It's a long story, and I promised Tom I'd meet him at the hospital. Please, can you just watch Katie until her mom comes? I'll tell you all about it later, okay?"

The other woman folded her arms across her chest, then agreed. As Gracie was slipping into her car, Cordelia shouted after her. "Want me to let Arnie know?"

Gracie poked her head out the window. "What?"

"You know, that whirling dervish. Arnie Houston."

"Why would he care about Tom?"

"Why they know each other!" Cordelia replied, Katie at her side. "They argue an awful lot, but I just thought Tom'd like to see a familiar face."

"I don't know," Gracie said, pulling away. As she drove to Keefer Memorial, Gracie ran through the list of questions she had for Tom Williams. She was tired of being lied to and upset that Tom would treat her friends, Anna and Joe, with such dishonesty. Especially as they were his only relatives. As she pulled in the parking lot Gracie realized she really did believe that Tom Williams was the Searfosses' nephew. Unfortunately, this revelation gave her no pleasure.

35

TOM'S EYES FLUTTERED OPEN. The doctor nodded to Gracie, who had been waiting for over an hour. "Not too long, okay? He needs rest."

She looked down at Tom, so vulnerable in the hospital bed. A hint of color was slowly returning to his face. Gracie's anger slipped away. The poor man was alone, sick and frightened, having just learned that he had a potentially life-threatening disease. "How are you feeling?"

He smiled slightly. "Better. It's a bit of a shock but much better." He licked his lips. She reached for the glass by his bed and helped him to drink. "Thank you. You're very kind, Mrs. Parks. I . . . I know I don't deserve it."

"Don't say that, Tom. You're human. We all make mistakes."

He turned his head away for a couple of minutes.

"Do you want me to leave?"

Tom's eyes flashed at her. "No! No, please. Stay. I was just thinking about your words." He sighed. "Guess not all mistakes are the same, huh?"

"In the eyes of the Lord, yes. That's really all that matters, Tom. And that you are sorry and willing to ask for forgiveness."

A single tear rolled down the side of his thin face. "I'm so sorry," he whispered. "You just don't know."

Gracie settled in her chair. "Do you want to tell me about it?"

He blinked slowly. "It . . . it's hard. I feel so stupid, almost dirty."

"Confession's good for the soul. I could call Pastor Paul Meyer, if you'd prefer?"

He tried to sit up but failed. "No! No . . . like you said, you're the one who deserves the truth. You and my aunt and uncle. May I have another drink?" She again offered the glass. He swallowed slowly, then smiled. "Guess I won't be drinking so much, once they get my blood sugar levels under control." He closed his eyes.

Nurse Bixler entered and took his pulse. "How're we feeling, Mr. Williams?"

"Tired."

"That's to be expected. Not much longer, Gracie, okay? Your uncle's waiting outside. Shall I send him in?"

Gracie rose and patted his shoulder. "You're tired and you've had a nasty shock. We can talk later."

"No!" Tom's eyes popped open. "Please, Nurse. I'm fine but don't let my uncle in, just yet, okay? Let Mrs. Parks stay a little longer. *Please*?"

Nancy Bixler raised her eyebrows then looked from her patient to Gracie. "Okay. A few more minutes."

"Thank you." He waited until she left. "Thank you, Mrs. Parks. I just can't face him yet. There's something . . . I . . . I need to get off my chest. Will you listen?"

"Of course, Tom."

Tom gathered his thoughts, then turned to Gracie. "First of all, you must believe me when I tell you I never meant to hurt my aunt or uncle. I really didn't know where they lived, Mrs. Parks, or anything about them. Not until the news clipping."

Gracie waited.

"It was like a gift. You see, I'm an agent."

"Like Arnie Houston."

His face tightened. "Well, not exactly."

"You pretended not to know him."

He nodded. "Had to. Didn't want to blow my cover." He sighed heavily. "You see, my business has been a bit rocky lately, some deals fell through. Clients had begun leaving. I was getting a little desperate when I saw the bit about my aunt." His expression brightened. "I knew she'd sign with me once she knew who I was. So . . ."

"Yes?"

He shrugged. "I made a deal with a production company. Said she was my client." He looked at her beseechingly. "Had to! I really needed the advance to cover some outstanding debts."

"You accepted an advance on your aunt's books without even first seeing her? Shame on you, Thomas Williams!"

He glanced out the window. "It was wrong. I know. I've felt bad ever since. Even worse when I realized how nice she is. And Uncle Joe. And how many friends they have, looking out for them. Guess I justified it by knowing how pleased they were to see me. I needed the money, I admit that's mostly why I came . . ." He shifted position. "I . . . I'd forgotten how good it was to have a family. But, once the lies got started, I didn't know how to stop them." He shuddered.

Gracie pulled the blanket over his shoulders.

"And then, Arnie stuck his big nose in, talking about a contract with my aunt before I could. And all heck breaks loose! The town thinks there's going to be a television series, my aunt feels she's responsible for making sure it happens . . . then, how could I tell her the truth?" His eyes were pleading, searching Gracie's. She squeezed his hand. "She'd only think I was doing it for the money, Mrs. Parks. Wouldn't blame her, but I wasn't." He sat up. "Honest! Not any more. Oh, I never meant for any of it to happen," Tom slouched back and yawned. "Like last night. That crazy old coot going at Uncle Joe. I felt so bad."

An ambulance rolled up to the emergency entrance, sirens blaring.

"Help me, Mrs. Parks. Please. I don't know what to do. There have been so many lies . . ." Tom's voice dropped then he hesitated. "If I tell the truth, I'm so afraid I'll lose Anna and Joe. I don't care any more about the money. I just want my family."

Gracie leaned forward and whispered. "Honesty's the best policy. Ask for God's help and trust in Him. He won't let you down."

Tom grasped her hand in gratitude.

"Now, you get some rest. Your uncle and aunt will want to see you. Make sure you're okay."

"Could you please tell them I'll talk to them soon? I . . ." his eyes fluttered. "I'm just going—"

Tom Williams fell asleep.

WHEN GRACIE LEFT TOM'S ROOM, she found both Joe and Anna, hand in hand, waiting outside. "Anna!" she exclaimed, embracing her dear friends. "Shouldn't you be in bed?"

Anna tried to smile. "I've been discharged. Joe was just about to take me home when we heard the ambulance. We heard someone say Tom's name so we stayed. We've been praying and waiting to see him. Is he all right?"

They sat back down on the couch. Gracie joined them. "He's fine. He's got to stay for a while."

Anna nodded. "He's a diabetic, too. Nurse Bixler told us." "Yes."

"Poor dear. It can be a cross to bear."

"He's luckier than most," Joe said. "He's under care and he's got you to show him the ropes."

"I never thought of it that way," Anna replied, her

expression brightening. "I could help him, couldn't I? It's not so bad once you get used to it."

"Of course, you can," Gracie said. "He's lucky to have you and Joe as family."

"Family," Anna whispered. "We're a family, Joe." Her husband gave her shoulders a gentle squeeze.

Nurse Bixler strode by. "Still waiting to see your nephew?"

Joe nodded.

"He's asleep," Gracie said.

"Good. He'll be right as rain in no time. Well, you know all about that, don't you, Anna?"

"May I just sit with him?" Anna asked. "I won't wake him."

The nurse hesitated, then took the elderly woman's hand. "Why not? I'm sure he'll be extremely glad to see your face when he wakes up."

Gracie turned to Joe. "I'm heading home. You're going to stay?"

He nodded. "Oh, Gracie, before you go. I got a call from the insurance company. Seems our fire at home was caused by faulty wiring in that new air conditioner. They're paying for everything. We should be able to move in in a week or so. If that's all right by you."

"I'm glad to hear the explanation for it is one that puts no blame on any person. What with all these strange little acts of arson. You know that you're both welcome for as long as you need. Okay? See you later, then," she said. "I'll ask that Tom's name be put on the prayer chain."

As she walked out of the hospital, Gracie gratefully took several deep breaths of fresh air. She glanced at her watch. It was late afternoon. Uncle Miltie would be frantic!

She quickly called home on her cell phone.

Her uncle answered on the first ring. "Gracie! Thank heavens you called, girl. Are you all right?"

As she explained what had transpired, she almost didn't believe it herself. So much had happened!

"So he really *is* Anna's nephew. A diabetic, huh? The apple doesn't fall far from the tree, does it? He going to be okay?"

"Yes. They're running some tests. Anna and Joe are waiting at the hospital."

"Oh, before I forget," her uncle said. "Phyllis Nickolson called. Wanted to thank you."

"Kate!" An idea flew into her head. "I totally forgot about her! Sorry, Uncle Miltie, I've got to go. I'll be home soon."

She hung up before he could reply and quickly dialed another number.

"Herb Bower, please. It's Gracie Parks."

"Oh, hello, Gracie! How's life treating you?"

"Just fine, Lucille. Uh, would you mind—"

"Sure. Just a minute."

Gracie waited for what seemed an eternity.

"He's on another line. Want to leave him a message?"

"No, thanks. Look, Lucille, could you just keep him there for a few minutes? I'm on my way from the hospital. I really need to see him."

"Hospital! Everything all right?"

"Fine. It's fine. Just hold onto him, would you? It's very important."

"Like glue, hon."

"Thanks for waiting for me, Herb."

The police chief rose, shook Gracie's hand over his desk, then motioned for her to sit. He followed suit, settling his large body into a leather chair. "Didn't have much choice. Lucille practically sat on me until you arrived."

Gracie felt a little light-headed while catching her breath. The sprint from the parking lot to the police station seemed very long.

"Can I get you something? Tea, coffee?"

Gracie realized that she was starving. "I'd love a coffee, thanks." She eyed a box on his desk. "You couldn't spare one of those cookies, could you? I haven't eaten since breakfast."

"Of course!" The big man jumped up, shouted the coffee request to Lucille, then handed Gracie the box. "Dive in. This about Arnie Houston?"

"Houston? No. Why?"

"Tell you later."

Gracie bit into the cookie and chewed, collecting her thoughts. "I know who the serial arsonist is."

Herb's body thrust forward. "You what?"

Gracie nodded, then swallowed. "Should have figured it out sooner. It's Phyllis Nickolson's daughter, Katie."

"Katie!" Herb exclaimed.

"Excuse me?" It was Lucille, standing in the doorway, a mug in her hands.

"Oh, sorry, Lucille. Come on in."

The dispatcher handed Gracie the coffee.

"But she's just a kid. Why'd do think she's the one setting the fires?"

Gracie finished her third cookie and sipped the hot coffee. "A bunch of little things. First, she fits your profile perfectly. Remember at Abe's you said that it was often kids, looking for thrills and attention? Well, Katie not only has a stepfather now, but a new brother who's stolen the limelight. I've seen the child. She's headstrong, making trouble in school, acting crazy around her mom, all sorts of things. The poor creature's desperate to be noticed. Secondly, she rides a bike. You found a tire track near my garage."

He nodded, munching a cookie.

Gracie took another sip of coffee. "Thirdly, my cat hissed at her. Gooseberry *never* does that. But I think he recognized her as the one who burned his tail." Herb raised his thick eyebrows. "And, lastly, I found her at Cordelia Fountain's a couple of hours ago with a half-spent book of matches in her hands."

Herb ran his tongue along the inside of his cheek. "That's that, then. Guess I'll have to go and talk to her and her parents." He shook his head. "The Nickolsons aren't going to like it."

"I don't think the child really meant any harm. She just didn't know the right way to show her anger. Isn't there anything you can do, Herb?"

He sighed. "How old's she?"

"Only eleven."

"I don't know. I'll have to think about it. Talk to her victims." He stood. "Really appreciate you coming in and telling me this, Gracie. Sorry to rush out but I'd better go, now. See her parents."

"Poor things," Gracie said, as she accompanied him out of the police station. "They're going to be so shocked."

37

SHE ARRIVED HOME to find her uncle and cat prowling the porch, waiting. She embraced Uncle Miltie, then picked up Gooseberry and gave him a big kiss and a hearty hug. "Oh, I've missed you two! Seems like I've been gone for ages."

"You have. It's nearly six o'clock."

"Good heavens! I didn't realize." She sniffed. "What's that? Fish?"

The elderly man grinned and pulled open the screen door with a flourish. "Enter, my dear. Supper awaits you."

And it did. Three lit candles flickered on the kitchen table. Two places were set, glasses of juice poured. Under covers were dishes filled with vegetable and shrimp dumplings, chicken with snow peas and fried rice.

"Chinese takeout! How wonderful!" she exclaimed, giving her uncle another buss on the cheek. "You read my mind. Oh, and I see some broccoli and water chestnuts, too."

He pulled her chair out for her then pushed it in when she sat. "Figured you'd be too tuckered to worry about dinner. Had Celestial City deliver it in a jiffy. There's enough for Joe, too, and Anna. He phoned to say he was bringing her home." He sat across from her. Gooseberry raced across the floor and jumped up onto the top of the fridge.

"Oh, this is so good! I'm absolutely famished." Gracie was already digging in.

"Eat, my dear. You can tell me all about the rest of your day later." He winked. "Over fortune cookies."

The doorbell rang.

"Oh, no!" Gracie groaned.

Uncle Miltie sighed. "I'll get it, my dear. Just keep eating."

A couple of moments later, Rocky Gravino strolled in. "Sorry to interrupt your dinner, Gracie."

"That's okay, Rocky. Have a dumpling."

He pulled up a chair and sat. "Already eaten, thanks." He eyed her plate. "Well, if you don't mind, maybe just one."

Uncle Miltie returned to his place, tugging his plate closer to his chest. He began quickly eating.

"Heard you had quite a day, Gracie," Rocky said, now spooning for himself a helping of rice. "Ran into Herb on his way to the Nickolsons. Thought you'd be interested in knowing that Arnie Houston's left town."

Gracie stopped chewing then swallowed. "He—" She

stopped, took a quick drink of juice then finished. "He left town? How? Why?"

Using his fork as a pointer, the editor said, "Hadn't told you yet, but I'd spoken to Herb about him."

"Oh!" Gracie suddenly remembered that the police chief hadn't gotten around to telling her his news about Houston.

"Pardon?"

"Uh, sorry, Rocky. It's not important. Go on."

"Well, our good police chief had a nice long chat with the young man. Told him he knew all about his shady practices and poor reputation and that he'd be informing Anna and Joe all about them as soon as possible."

"What'd he do?" Uncle Miltie asked, able to pay attention now that most of his meal was safely in his stomach.

Rocky laughed heartily. "You should hear Herb tell it." He stood up for emphasis and deepened his voice in a parody of Willow Bend's chief of police. "Punk takes another look at me. I'm at least six inches taller. Outweigh him by about sixty pounds. He eyes my gun, then the police cruiser behind me. Sirens still going. Then he did what any crook would do in his situation. He hightailed it." Rocky laughed again, sat down and continued in his own voice. "Herb followed him to Cordelia's, waited until he paid up, then escorted him to the outskirts of town." He wasn't happy, but he's gone.

"Sounds a bit like the wild west," Gracie said, dabbing her lips with a napkin.

"Got what he deserved, if you ask me," Rocky replied.

"Well. That was wonderful, Uncle Miltie. Thank you very much. It was very thoughtful."

His blue eyes twinkled.

"How about a coffee?" she asked Rocky.

"Thought you'd never ask."

"Anyone home?" Joe's voice could be heard in the hallway.

"Joe! Anna!" Gracie replied, jumping up. She and Rocky helped Anna negotiate the doorway and led her to a kitchen chair. "Are you hungry? Uncle Miltie had Celestial City send over a feast!"

"Starved. But we've got a surprise."

Tom Williams's head popped in the door.

"Tom!" Gracie cried. "Come in! Aren't you supposed to be in the hospital?"

Tom walked to a chair and sunk down. "They let me go early. Have to go back tomorrow for some more tests but . . ."

"Well, how wonderful to see you all!" Gracie started examining her kitchen counter where the leftovers sat in their serving dishes. "I think we might have enough here for a start. I can rustle up something else."

"I'm sure it'll be enough," Joe said. "Tom and Anna ate a little at the hospital."

Gracie dished chicken and broccoli onto three plates, which Rocky handed around. He then disappeared into the dining room and returned with another chair.

"Aren't we blessed!" Gracie said, as they all settled around her table. "To have you all here, safe and sound."

Everyone took a moment to give thanks.

T HE DOORBELL RANG AGAIN.

"Good grief!" Uncle Miltie exclaimed. "Might as well leave that thing standing wide open. It's not a door, it's a vertical welcome mat!"

Gracie went to answer the bell, Gooseberry trotted at her heels. "Why, hello, Herb! Come on in. We were just talking about you."

"Only the good parts, right?"

The others warmly greeted the police chief. Rocky offered to fetch another chair.

"In a minute, if you don't mind. Gracie?"

Taking the hint, Gracie led him into the living room. Her cat took up his position of vigilance on the sofa.

"I just wanted to let you know what the Nickolsons and I've agreed on."

"Please, sit down."

Once settled, Herb continued. "I've spoken to Katie, her parents and the individuals she targeted. Katie admitted to setting all the fires except the one at the Searfosses. Not surprising, really. It didn't really fit the pattern."

"Oh, I forgot to say. Joe told me earlier this afternoon. Their fire was caused by faulty wiring in a new air conditioning system they'd had installed."

Herb nodded. "Well, that solves that big part of the puzzle. Anyway, back to our junior arsonist. I think we've arrived at a pretty fair settlement, for all concerned."

Gracie leaned forward.

"The Nickolsons have accepted responsibility for her actions. They're going to pay for all the damages and get Katie some counseling in exchange for our not charging her. The little girl's also going to help out an hour or so at Abe's, Anderson's and Barry's."

"That's a good idea."

"Would you like her to come here, as well?"

Gracie shook her head. "I think she'll learn more with the others."

"Okay, but this community service is real important. Allows her to meet and know the folks she's harmed."

"I think that's very fair, Herb. I thank you for coming here to tell me."

The big man rose. "Figured you deserved to know, seeing

how she nearly burned down your garage, and, more importantly, you're the one who discovered that she was the culprit."

"Seems I have more to thank you for," Gracie added, standing.

"Huh?"

She smiled and took his arm. "You scared the daylights out of Arnie Houston and saved Anna and Joe a lot of heartache."

A grin spread across his face. "Oh that!" He made a mock bow and replied in a western twang. "Nothing to it, ma'am. Just doing my job. I'd say he wanted to leave. Kept sneezing and mumbling about how he didn't like smalltown vibes."

Gracie laughed at the image. "Well, I'm very grateful, sir. Come on in and sit down with us for a cup of coffee."

She was still laughing as they entered the noisy kitchen.

Marge was now sitting there and shouted out a hello. "Heard the hullabaloo. Had to come over to see what was up."

Gracie gave her neighbor a quick hug and dropped into an empty seat.

"Oh, Gracie," Joe pushed a tall, beautifully wrapped rectangular package across the table. "This's for you."

Gracie glanced at Anna and Joe. Her uncle caught her eye and grinned. The rest of her guests smiled.

"There's no way to repay your kindness or courage," Anna

said, in a soft voice, "but Joe and I hoped you would accept this small gift as a token of our thanks and friendship."

"Oh, Anna and Joe, you didn't have to!" Gracie exclaimed.

Anna reached out and found Gracie's hand. "Open it, please."

Gracie fumbled with the tape but managed to rip the colorful wrapping off. "Your books!" she exclaimed, her hands gripping the hard covers.

Anna beamed. "An original copy of each Lazy Lake title."

"Look inside," Joe urged. "They're autographed."

Gracie flipped open the first book, recognized Anna's looping signature, and silently read the acknowledgment. A lump formed in her throat.

"What's it say?" Uncle Miltie asked.

Tears filled Gracie's eyes. She shook her head and handed him the book.

"For our dear friend, Gracie Parks," her uncle read. "Her ways are ways of pleasantness, and all her paths are peace. Proverbs 17."

"That's so beautiful!" Marge exclaimed, handing Gracie a tissue.

"Oh, Anna and Joe!" Gracie cried, while wiping her eyes. She rose, and gave each a long embrace. "I'm so blessed to have you as friends." She paused for a moment, collecting her thoughts. "I read something in *Guideposts* once that really touched me. I'd like to share it with you now. 'Some fragrance must remain on the hand that gives you roses.' Thank you, Anna and Joe, for your wonderful gift!"

It was the Searfosses' turn to become emotional. Tears glistening on their faces, they hugged each other and then Gracie.

The others clapped heartily. Both Marge and Uncle Miltie reached for a tissue.

"May I?" Herb asked. He reached out to take a book from Gracie's pile.

Gracie nodded.

"We've got Ann O'Neill to thank for that one," Joe said. "When I went looking through our shelves for extras, I discovered that we were missing one volume. Ann's mother kindly gave us her copy to give to you."

"Oh, but she shouldn't have!" Gracie replied. "Are you sure?"

He nodded. "She was delighted. Anna signed the rest of her copies and promised her a replacement from the first edition of the new run."

"How kind of her!" Gracie said. "I'll give her a call to thank her personally."

For a while, everyone concentrated on the books, with each person reading snippets aloud and admiring the charming illustrations.

Gracie slipped over to Tom. "Everything all right?"

He stopped sipping apple juice and smiled. "Couldn't be better, Mrs. Parks. Told them the whole story. Just as you suggested." He reached out and grabbed his aunt's hand. "And they've forgiven me. Aren't I lucky?"

"We all are, son," Joe replied. "We all are."

"Can you imagine?" Anna asked. "My nephew, Tommy. A literary agent. He's been in the business for years. Isn't that something! He's going to represent me."

"Yes," replied Gracie, meaning it. "Wonderful."

"She asked me," Tom quickly added. "I didn't offer."

Joe smiled. "Of course you'll represent her! Why, she's your own flesh and blood, young man."

"I'm pretty certain I can negotiate a very attractive deal with the cable networks myself," his nephew continued. "With all this excitement, they'll be lining up to get her books. Nothing's signed until my aunt's certain she likes the approach. And we'll talk about a shooting location, right, Auntie Anna?"

Anna beamed.

Gooseberry curled through Gracie's legs. She reached down to stroke him.

"Here, here!" Uncle Miltie boomed.

"A toast!" Rocky said, rising to his feet, right arm outstretched. "To Anna and Joe Searfoss."

"Anna and Joe!" the others echoed, all standing.

Everyone grinned.

"Our dear friends. May good health and good fortune continue to bless you all the days of your lives."

"Amen!" replied his enthusiastic chorus.

Gracie's Broccoli-and-Cheese Omelet

- ✓ 1 cup broccoli, steamed and cut into small pieces
- ✓ 5 eggs
- ✓ 2 tablespoons milk
- ✓ pinch of salt and freshly ground pepper
- ✓ 2 tablespoons butter
- ✓ 1/3 cup seasoned salad croutons (optional)
- ✓ 1/3 cup shredded sharp Cheddar cheese
- ✓ pinch of paprika (optional)

Steam one to two stems broccoli (depending on size) until just barely tender. Cut into moderately small pieces to make one cup and set aside.

Break eggs into a bowl, add milk and beat with a fork. Add salt and pepper, and continue to beat. In well-seasoned cast-iron frying pan, melt butter over low heat. Add croutons and brown while butter is melting, if desired.

Pour in egg mixture, retaining low heat. Immediately begin to lift the edges and bottom as eggs set, then distribute cheese over surface, reserving a little. Next sprinkle broccoli over cheese, all the while gently loosening omelet from pan. Add reserved cheese, turn off heat and remove from burner. Lightly dust with paprika, if desired.

Wait a few minutes until omelet is firm before cutting into wedges. Makes two servings, depending on side dishes and appetites.

Gracie says, "It's important not to overcook the broccoli. It won't look as pretty or taste as good if it's mushy! My cheese preference is for a tangy white Cheddar, but a yellow one will work equally well. Asparagus can be substituted for the broccoli. The croutons, I think, add an interesting texture contrast. Hash browns always go well with an omelet, but sometimes I make oven-baked 'fries' instead. A cinnamon-y baked apple makes a nice finish to the meal!"

About the Author

NICOLA FURLONG makes every effort to steal time away from cycling, playing ice hockey, growing perennials from seed and devouring chocolates (mostly devouring chocolates) to slip a snippet of mystery and suspense writing into each day.

Born in Edmonton, Alberta, the sixth of eight children, Nicola was raised in the Canadian provinces of Saskatchewan, Ontario and Prince Edward Island. She received a degree in fine arts and psychology from Carleton University in Ottawa, and then, following several older siblings, scrambled up the bureaucratic ladder with the Canadian government. After the publication of a number of essays, articles and short stories, her first mystery novel, *Teed Off!*, was published in 1996. Later that year, she left the civil service behind to concentrate on writing fiction and also serving as a consultant to fisheries and environmental organizations. Her second novel, *A Hemorrhaging of Souls*, was published in 1998. She recently finished a suspense thriller entitled *Thy Will Be Done* and is currently researching a sequel.

Nicola lives in Sidney-by-the-Sea, a small town on southern Vancouver Island, British Columbia, with Brodie, a West Highland white terrier, and Sammy, a cream-colored Persian cat. You can visit her Web site at www.nicolafurlong.com.

A NOTE FROM THE EDITORS

This original Guideposts book was created by the Book and Inspirational Media Division of the company that publishes *Guideposts*, a monthly magazine filled with true stories of people's adventures in faith.

Guideposts is available by subscription. All you have to do is write to Guideposts, 39 Seminary Hill Road, Carmel, New York 10512. When you subscribe, each month you can count on receiving exciting new evidence of God's presence, His guidance and His limitless love for all of us.

Guideposts is also available on the Internet by accessing our home page on the World Wide Web at www.guideposts.org. Send prayer requests to our Monday morning Prayer Fellowship. Read stories from recent issues of our magazines, *Guideposts, Angels on Earth, Guideposts for Kids,* and *Guideposts for Teens,* and follow our popular book of devotionals, *Daily Guideposts.* Excerpts from some of our best-selling books are also available.